D0436259

THE

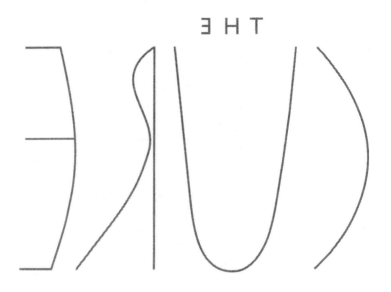

THE CURE

BY
SONIA
LEVITIN

Silver Whistle
HARCOURT BRACE & COMPANY
SAN DIEGO   NEW YORK   LONDON

Library of Congress Cataloging-in-Publication Data
Levitin, Sonia, 1934–
The cure/by Sonia Levitin.
p. cm.
"Silver Whistle."
Summary: A sixteen-year-old boy living in 2407 collides with the past when he finds himself
in Strasbourg in 1348 confronting the anti-Semitism that sweeps through Europe during the
Black Plague.
ISBN 0-15-201827-1
[1. Antisemitism—Fiction. 2. Prejudices—Fiction. 3. Jews—Europe—Fiction. 4. Black
death—Fiction. 5. Middle Ages—Fiction. 6. Time travel—Fiction.] I. Title.
PZ7.L58Cu 1999
[Fic]—dc21   98-33907

Text set in Meredien Medium
Designed by Judythe Sieck
First edition

F E D C B

Printed in the United States of America

To my grandmothers, Lucie Goldstein and Rosa Wolff,
among the many martyrs.
You are loved and cherished and remembered.

ACKNOWLEDGMENTS

My heartfelt gratitude to the following for their kind help with this book: Professor John Allman, California Institute of Technology; Jane Arnault; Rita Frischer, Sinai Temple Library, Los Angeles; Paul Hamburg; Adaire Klein, Director of Library and Archival Services, Simon Wiesenthal Center and Museum of Tolerance; Dr. Daniel J. Levitin; Professor Steven M. Lowenstein, University of Judaism; Professor Sharon Snowiss, Claremont College; Joel Tuchman, Sinai Temple Library, Los Angeles; and Professor Amnon Yariv, California Institute of Technology.

PROLOGUE

From the merchant ships anchored at the docks, bobbing and swaying in the churning sea, from the ships' cargo being hoisted ashore—casks and crates and piles of hemp—the rats emerged.

Rattus rattus, *the common species, dark brown and fretful, crawled out along the docks, into bins of flour and spices and bundles of cloth. The rats twitched and itched from the bites of insatiable fleas. The rats—having traveled far, from Cathay and India and other mysterious lands—came ashore carrying their own deadly cargo.*

—1348, Genoa, Italy

CHAPTER
ONE

Again that dream! How was it possible to dream of things one had never experienced? Gemm 16884 turned on his anti-gravity bed, propped himself up on one elbow, and gazed at the screen, which reflected date, time, and the Morning Message.

He wished his twin, Gemma 16884, were here. Tonight he would ask her to sleep with him instead of with her girlfriends. They would lie close. With Gemma beside him, there would be no troubling dreams.

For several months this same dream had recurred, and afterward he was left with feelings of weakness and an odd yearning. In the dream he stood atop the artificial red-rock mountains. Strange desires surged through him. His breathing was rapid, his mind racing relentlessly on rhythms and sounds. The sounds came from some space inside him that he did not know, but they were beautiful and overwhelming. In the dream Gemm 16884 gazed up at the starry sky, and he let the sounds flow from him, and he felt lifted up and free. The rhythm captivated him, making his body move and twist in ways that were surely forbidden. Never had he seen or heard anyone do this. It frightened him.

He had, of course, heard rumors of people having peculiar seizures—flashes, they were called. Gemm 16884 shuddered. Everything was going so well. He and his twin were about to make the Great Choice. Surely they had followed every edict rigorously. He and Gemma were superior in health and intellect. They were in their prime. No, nothing could go wrong.

Gemm leaned toward the low hum of the screen. Its vibrations were steady and soothing, while his dream had been as exciting as a session at the Joy Drome. But, of course, nobody remembered exactly what happened at the Joy Drome; only the feeling remained, a quiet exultation. His dream was different; the memory of it did not fade.

Last week, after the dream had come again, he asked the Leader of their quadrant whether it was possible to dream the unimagined and unknown.

Leader 77520 had rubbed his jaw and tapped his knuckles together rapidly. "Of course not," he replied staunchly. The Leader's number encircled the neck band of his gold jumpsuit. Gemm did not know his familiar name, and he felt too self-conscious to ask. "The brain stores only that to which it has been exposed, and we know that dreams come from the brain's activity." Leader 77520 pressed his fingertips to his temples, securing his mask. It was pearl gray with full, dark eyebrows, giving the leader a studious look. "What was this dream about?" he asked.

"Oh, nothing," Gemm replied, turning away. "Only some nonsense. I don't really remember it very well."

"In friendship and love," said Leader 77520, "I would advise you to seek analysis."

"In love," replied Gemm 16884, "I thank you. Perhaps I will." Gemm took a deep breath, steadying his heartbeat. Actually, he had no intention of going through that process.

Leader 77520 seemed to read his thoughts. "You know, you could use Med Com for a printout. Isn't it near time for your Great Choice? You don't want anything to interfere now, do you?"

"Indeed," said Gemm with a deferential nod, adding, "In love, I thank you."

Leader 77520 took a step toward Gemm. "Get yourself a serotonin shake," he advised. "You seem a bit flashed."

Gemm noticed that the Leader had already documented the conversation, pressing the com button on his cuff. Gemm 16884 bent deep from his waist. He wished he hadn't spoken at all, but then, that's what the Leaders were there for, wasn't it? And it was perverse to keep secrets. "Tranquillity reigns," said Leader 77520 in dismissal.

"Tranquillity begets Peace," Gemm responded.

Leader 77520 touched Gemm's shoulders. The sudden warmth had startled Gemm, and it was infinitely comforting. He had felt better immediately.

Now Gemm lowered his antigravity bed and approached the screen, holding his wrist to the scanner, at the same time reporting, "Gemm 16884, free day, pleasure scents and scenes, company of twin and several others."

The screen voice intoned, "Name others please."

"Kir and Kira, maybe some others."

"Numbers, numbers," prompted the screen voice.

"Look them up," Gemm said, feeling slightly irritated. He needed to get to the breakfast bar. If Gemma heard him sounding irritable, she would coax him to get a scan, and he didn't want to take the time. He had looked forward to this day of leisure, away from tests and instruction; and he was entitled to it! Indeed, as he stood waiting for the machine's response he heard the atmospheric whisper, "Fourth day free. Shout praises!"

"Looking, looking," droned the machine; and then, "Registered. You are excused. May you experience pleasure."

"In love, I thank you," Gemm responded, and turned into the hygienic passageway, soothed by the warm and fragrant mist. He stood for a few extra seconds under the drying lamp, then pulled on his jumpsuit. He was aware of others beside him, also engaging in the morning cleansing, but of course he kept his eyes averted as he stood before the reflector, adjusting his mask.

The mask was one of the more conservative models, a delicate peach shade with scarcely any eyebrows and short brown hair of fine silk. Gemm had been wearing the same mask for months, without any thought of changing. Somehow, now, he desired a different face. He looked through the rack, but nothing really pleased him. Well, the new models were coming out in a month. Gemma, like the other girls, was terribly excited about it. She would stand in front of the purchase screen for hours making her choice. Last time he pretended to be interested only for her sake. Now, in truth, he was eager for something new. So many choices! He thought: *A thousand choices!* It occurred to him briefly that only twelve masks were ever available. Whenever a new model was introduced, an old one was recalled. Well, it was only a saying. And most things *did* come in thousands. *A thousand choices.* The words hummed through his mind. Gemm 16884 found his spirits lifting. "Shout praises," he murmured.

He strode through the main hall to the loggia, where Gemma usually waited for him in the mornings. Passageways opened and closed; the synthetic roof provided varieties of clouds, fragrances, and colors. Atmospheric whispers accompanied Gemm's progress: "Day of pleasure . . . Day of one thousand choices . . . Tranquillity is peace." Suddenly the rhythm and the sounds from his dream intervened; Gemm quickened his steps, determined to banish them.

He found Gemma and Kira engrossed in talk, with Kir and several of the others standing nearby, playing one of the new multi-dimensional puzzles. Most of their quadrant mates still wore the pale yellow jumper, with their birth numbers printed in black on the front. A few of their friends had already graduated to colors of choice, depending on their careers.

He could hear Gemma and her friend Kira as he approached. Kira was laughing, as usual, her tone bright and saucy. "Kir and I tested out to be either athletic technicians or keepers of the robot zoo. Can you imagine anything more diverse?"

"Not really," Gemma replied with a slight laugh. "Both involve mechanical knowledge. You and Kir are such gifted mechanics. Everyone admires you."

"No, you are most admired," protested Kira, but she sounded quite pleased.

The two girls stood with their arms linked. Gemma was slightly taller and slimmer than Kira. Of course, they were all from the same birth batch, all friends of the highest order. Kira and Gemma usually chose the same masks, pale bronze in color, with exaggerated eye openings outlined in lavender—quite nice, Gemm thought. "Pleasant morning," Gemm greeted everyone.

"May it please you," they responded.

"Ready for your breakfast?" Gemm asked.

"If it pleases you," Gemma replied, motioning to the others.

A group of girls from the next higher quadrant crossed their path, talking animatedly. "It's really fun to see them starting to develop," one exclaimed. "Darling little things—were we ever that small?"

"All alike as peas in a pod," said another. "What I remember most are the parties, all the special things . . ."

Kira and Gemma drew close to their twins. "They've all done it already," Gemma said with a touch of envy in her voice. "See how their new bracelets shine!"

"In a few months you'll be there, too," Gemm assured her.

"They say it doesn't hurt," Kira said hopefully.

"I'm sure it doesn't," Kir said. "I've heard it's just a slight discomfort, and only for a day or two."

"Look who's talking!" The girls laughed a little nervously. "Boys always say it doesn't hurt. How would they know?"

"Well, we'll be wearing the gold, though," Gemma said, raising her wrist with the wide birth bracelet of silver, which, after parenting, would be changed to gold. "I love gold," she said.

"Everyone does," said Kira. "People used to fashion gold into different things."

"Wherever did you hear that?" asked Gemma, shocked.

"It came on the screen; a Folk Fact. It said that in Past Time people used to collect ornaments and—they even made coins and exchanged them for—well, for the ornaments and—," Kira stammered. "Different things, I guess."

"Why would they want different things?" Gemma demanded, her hands braced on her hips. "Diversity begets hostility."

"I know that," said Kira. "It's just a Folk Fact. It's amusing."

"Quite so," Gemma agreed. They drifted toward the Serotonin Bar.

"You slept well?" Gemm inquired. He leaned toward Gemma,

wishing—he wasn't certain what he wished for. He found himself remembering the dream, the rhythm. He glanced to the side, where a Scooper was making its way along the turf with a series of sounds; *rumm-humm-clicka-clicka*. It drew his attention, so that he scarcely heard Gemma's reply. *Rumm-humm-clicka-clicka*. In his mind the beat repeated.

Gemma said, "I always sleep well after a night at the Drome. And you?"

"Please sleep with me tonight, Gemma."

"Of course, if it will pleasure you."

They walked on for several moments, raising their hands in greeting to the other pairs converging from the many paths leading to the Serotonin Bar.

"I had that dream again." His heart pounded fiercely from indecision. Should he tell her everything? If anyone could understand, it was Gemma. They were twins, mated for life, genetically matched, born for each other. And yet, there were differences. As hard as he tried to match her desires, there were differences. His dreams were but one example.

"What was in the dream?" Gemma asked casually. She waved to several friends. Her silver armband, with its birth number, 16884, glowed in the sunlight.

"That's just it," Gemm replied. "I hardly know how to describe it. I was in a large place, like the Joy Drome, and all around me were vibrations, and my body was moving, and my voice made sounds like—like a chant, but different."

"You mean the screen was vibrating, don't you? The atmosphere was whispering, chanting . . ."

"No! It was I! I—I felt different." He shook his head and lifted his arms helplessly. "I don't know. I feel—well, perplexed."

"Get a double drink for breakfast," Gemma said soothingly.

"But it was the same dream I've had many times before!"

"Dreams are quickly forgotten," Gemma said, hastening her steps. Gemm pulled her back. "Not this one," he said. "I remember it."

They had reached the Serotonin Bar. Gemm swiftly passed his wrist number over the scanner, recalling Kira's comment about gold.

It *was* amusing. He had seen a Folk Fact about ancient coins made of gold. People used them to pay for things. There were no wrist numbers and automatic debits. He glanced at the screen. It blinked FLAVOR CHOICE rapidly in green letters. "Shout praises," he murmured in genuine gratitude.

"Shout praises," Gemma responded reverently.

"What would you like?" Gemm 16884 asked Gemma 16884.

"I don't know. Let me think. So many choices. A thousand choices . . ."

"A thousand choices," he responded indulgently. Indeed, row upon row of icons invoked every possible flavor, both natural and synthetic. Gemma finally selected the flavor Gemm knew she would, platinum pecan. "May it pleasure you," he said.

"And you," she replied.

He heard the relentless beat of the Scooper as it sanitized the turf, *rumm-humm-clicka-clicka*. Unconsciously, Gemm snapped his fingers in rhythm to the Scooper.

"Stop it," said Gemma 16884.

"What?"

"You know. That snapping. It's harsh," she said, turning away from him.

"Sorry." Gemm thrust his hands into his sash. He bent toward his twin and said softly, "Look, maybe you and I could go alone to the country, just this once."

She spun around. "Whatever for? Kir and Kira and some others . . ."

"Never mind." Gemm 16884 shook himself. "It was just a notion." The beat of the Scooper pulsed within him, like something imprisoned, needing release.

"Are you feeling quite well? You haven't even chosen your drink. Maybe you should check with Med Com."

"I'm fine!" Swiftly Gemm punched in a mixed flavor, volcanic cinnamon spice. In moments the drink, bubbling and fragrant, poured into a cup.

Gemma scratched the back of her neck. Gemm could see wisps of reddish hair escaping under her mask. Quickly she tucked them back and fluffed out the silky bronze strands that hung down her back. "What flavor's that?" she asked.

He gave her a sip. She spat it out. Immediately the Scooper came by and sucked up the liquid. "Horrible!" she cried. "What's the matter with you, Gemm 16884? You always get either apricot zest or almond alloy."

"Can't a person make a change?"

"Of course you can!" she cried. "A thousand choices . . ."

Kir and Kira came up to them, arms linked and steps matched. "Let's go," said Kira.

"Let's do the real animal zoo," said Kir.

"If it pleasures you," said Gemm. He slid his wrist number over the scanner in the archway, punched in their destination: REAL ANIMAL ZOO.

"Last time we went," said Kira in a whisper, "did I tell you what happened?" She gave a slight giggle. "Those dogs?"

"I remember," said Kir, his tone stern. "We went with Zo and Zoa and some others. I had no idea . . . I mean . . ." He lowered his voice. "They were coupling."

"Coupling!" Gemm 16884 exclaimed. "Why didn't you tell me?"

"It was too disgusting," said his friend. He cleared his throat.

"People used to do it!" Kira chirped.

"Stop it, Kira," said her twin. "Be nice. We're out for a day of pleasure. After the zoo we can go to the red-rock mountains and climb."

Kira laughed. "Why go to all that trouble? I'd just as soon do the muscle manipulator—less work."

The two girls were whispering together. Gemm 16884 knew they were talking about the animals coupling and how people used to take pleasure in—he couldn't even say the words to himself, and he felt his face burning beneath the mask.

High in the sky a bird circled, sending down a piercing sound, long and wavering.

Gemm stared up at the bird, his heart pounding in alarm. He wanted to run, to soar, and to call out something high pitched and wavering, long and lovely, as he had done in his dream. Deep inside his breast, a feeling surged, beating like the wings of that bird, longing for release. He wanted . . . he wanted . . . he had no name for it, but it was like the bird and the Scooper and his dream.

"Gemm 16884!" called his twin. "Come on! What are you looking at?"

But Gemm 16884 could not pull himself away from the vision of that bird, its beautiful sounds, and the desires it aroused in him. He found himself swaying, shoulders and arms moving in rhythm to an inner sound not unlike the call of the bird. *"Ah, la—la-la-la—ah, eee-doo!"*

As the sounds flowed from him, Gemm's entire being loosened, as if he had been chained and was now suddenly released. *"Ah . . . ah . . . lo . . . lo . . . la . . . dee . . . dee . . . oh!"*

Swiftly the others surrounded him. They laid him down on the turf, their faces very near his. One hand clasped his pulse, the other his throat.

"Get him to the compound."

"Quick, we have to put him on Med Com."

"Should we call for assistance? For transport?"

"Get away!" Gemm 16884 shouted. "Leave me alone. I don't need anyone!"

Still they pressed upon him. "Hush, what's come over you? Those monstrous noises!"

"Leave me alone! I want . . . I need to . . ." He lifted his chin and let the sounds roar from his chest, the glad and free and lovely sounds. *"La . . . la . . . la . . . dum . . . da . . . da!"*

They reached out to console him. Gemm pushed them away, hard. They fell back, crying out in shock. Pushing was not allowed. Anger and hostility were unheard of, except in small children before they were trained to tranquillity. What had he done? Gemm 16884 moved away from the others, walking backward. They watched him, stunned. Gemma's hands covered her mouth. Kira began to cry.

Kir reached out. "In love, we will get you some help." Kir's fingers grazed the com button on his cuff.

"I need nothing!" Gemm 16884 cried. "Leave me alone!" He bent down and picked up an artificial red rock and threw it. The rock grazed Kir's head, then landed on the ground and disintegrated completely. A smear of blood seeped along the edge of Kir's mask, staining his yellow jumper. Gemma screamed.

Now, hysterically, Kir summoned help, touching his com button. "Request immediate assistance!"

Fear gripped Gemm. "Kir! Kira and Gemma, listen," Gemm cried out. "In love, I ask forgiveness. Please don't call them! Don't let them take me."

In moments, four transporters arrived in the hover-shuttle. The four, dressed in the grim black and red, rushed toward Gemm 16884 and took him away.

CHAPTER TWO

G emm heard them talking about him. He felt as if he were in a tunnel, or at the Joy Drome right after the vibrations and the color-noise stopped. Then, there was always a moment of dazed incomprehension as ecstasy abated and the body returned to its natural flow.

Now Gemm felt confused and a little afraid. The medic continued to question Gemma and their friends.

"Has this sort of thing happened before? This sudden aggression?"

"No, of course not," answered Kir. "He is passive, always, and tranquil."

"Do you know what triggered the outburst? Did he have his serotonin shake this morning?"

"Yes!" exclaimed Gemma. "We all had breakfast together."

"When was he last scanned?"

"We go every month, according to regulation!" Gemma's voice rang out sharply. Gemm 16884 heard the panic in his twin's tone. If either of them were found deficient, they would not be allowed to parent. Gemma would be devastated. Not to parent, except by choice, was almost as bad as being a Single.

Gemm opened his eyes and saw that Med Com was attached to his upper arms.

The medic turned to Gemma and said sharply, "Easy now, Fem 16884, or we might suspect that his condition is contagious."

"In love," Gemma replied quickly, "I ask forgiveness."

"Granted."

Gemm 16884 spoke up. "I also beg forgiveness of those I have offended."

"Granted," said Kir and Kira in unison, and the medic murmured his forgiveness, too.

Gemm saw his bodily signs registering on the screen. He took a deep breath, using the control techniques they had learned as small children. Monitors recorded his pulse and brain activity, hormone level, and a dozen other indicators of health and mood. Of course, he could not alter his blood chemistry, but with biofeedback techniques he could regulate his mood. He let the mantra flood his mind: *Conformity begets Harmony. . . .*

"Ah, he's calming down," said the medic. "Good. Just a few months now before your Great Choice, isn't it? That can be stressful. Then, the parenting—the parties, all the decisions about food, colors, entertainment . . ." As he spoke the medic carefully noted the readout. Gemm saw that the indicators were leveling off now. Good.

"Yes, I'm sure that's what it was," Gemm said. He recalled having been given some kind of injection when the transporters took him—probably serotonin concentrate. He was feeling peaceful now—mellow, well-o. The rhythmic murmuring of the Med Com caught his attention, intruding on his reverie. With effort, Gemm turned his mind toward the mantra, the Ladder of Five: *Conformity begets Harmony begets Tranquillity begets Peace begets Universal Good. Shout Praises!*

The medic stood over Gemm, panning his reflexes with the sonar scope. Casually he said, "Your twin told us something about a dream."

"I'm willing to take medication," Gemm said. "I beg forgiveness . . ."

"And in the dream you were making certain sounds—music?" The medic coughed slightly to hide his embarrassment. "Do you understand what you did? Do you know the law?"

"Indeed I do," replied Gemm hastily.

"And that you asked for privacy today. Is that so?"

"I just thought . . . it was foolish and perverse," said Gemm. "I've been working too hard, getting ready for career choice."

The medic coded the data into Gemm's file. His mask, snow white with a blue nose and pointed blue eyebrows, was usually the style favored by teachers or enforcers, designed to amuse the children and banish concern. Gemm wondered how the medic might look with his mask removed. Instantly he was seized with alarm. A loud *bleep* came from the computer; the medic started.

"My, my. Something is certainly going on here. Dramatic shift in hormone level. Look, I am not an enforcer, only a medic. But I advise you to control these outbursts. You have been taught better. You know that venting such . . . such passions denies tranquillity, arousing instead . . . well, we need not speak of it. Music." He spoke the word with loathing. "Really, I am surprised. Nobody else in your birth batch has such notions."

With a mighty effort, Gemm 16884 brought his thoughts and his bodily signs under control. The screen hummed softly, a purring sound.

The medic rubbed the side of his mask, pulled his chin. "Well, it might only be the stress of choices. However," he added firmly, "I want you to come in at once should you have a recurrence. These things must be short-circuited at once. Do you understand?"

"We understand," said Gemm and Gemma in unison.

"I'm giving you a prescription for Meltonite, which you are to take each evening before you retire. It will not banish dreams," the medic continued, "but it will provide more acceptable visions. Understood?"

"Understood," said Gemm. "In love, I thank you."

The medic rolled up the Med Com cable, gave the machine a shove with his foot, and nodded. "Peace."

"Tranquillity," said Gemm and Gemma.

"The incident is forgotten," said Kir in a kind tone.

"Most certainly," echoed Kira.

Gemm 16884 found his eyes smarting. A tenderness stirred inside him, a feeling of wanting and wishing—he did not know what it was. He only knew that it did not belong. So Gemm 16884 smoothed his mask, lifted his shoulders, and strode ahead, making his tone robust. "Let's go to the red-rock mountains! There's still time. Then to the scent tent. Come on, friends!"

. . .

It was one of those fine nights when Gemma lay beside him on the antigravity bed, and they talked and talked, and Gemma pressed her fingertips to Gemm's face, and he felt the slight pressure and warmth of her fingers through his mask.

Along with their quadrant mates from the same birth batch, the twins shared a certain apprehension. Sixteen was almost upon them. Sixteen, the year of Great Choices.

"Tell me what you want," Gemm 16884 said to Gemma 16884 as she lay beside him. Fragrances drifted around them. Warm mist lay like a moving blanket over their bodies.

"I want to parent," Gemma said earnestly. "I do want the gold. Is that wrong?"

"Of course not," Gemm said. "It's your gift for going through the process."

"I'm afraid," Gemma said softly. "I'm afraid that it might hurt."

"You know that isn't so," Gemm said. "They'll give you medications. You can watch the entire process on the screen."

"I don't want to watch."

"Then you don't have to."

"I do want to do my share," Gemma said. "For the universal good. I want to contribute my eggs."

"Then you shall. Look, afterward we'll go to the Womb Room and watch the fetuses. They say it's very interesting. Often the twins are already touching. They are like one being."

"Like us," Gemma said. "Your pleasure is my pleasure."

"Exactly. Probably you and I touched in the Womb Room. You and I have always desired the same things and felt the same feelings." But something intruded in Gemm's thoughts, like a warning. For months he and Gemma had agreed that they would follow a technical career. For one thing, Gemma loved the purple jumpers of the techs; for another, they had both proved their aptitude for working with machines, especially in the area of transportation. Now tentatively he murmured, "I've been thinking what it might be like to be a . . . a teacher. Don't you like their checked jumpers?"

He felt Gemma stiffen. "I thought we had decided that we would train for the flight operations."

"I know. I just thought—"

"It's so dull being a teacher," Gemma said. "I wouldn't want to spend time with children. They're so noisy and they have to be trained. I'd hate it, Gemm. Of course, if it pleases you . . ."

From the screen came a *bleep*, then a flash—FOLK FACT: "In Past Time people died at various ages and were actually forbidden to choose recycling!" Another *bleep*, and the image and audio abruptly vanished.

"Imagine that!" Gemma exclaimed.

"What?"

"In Past Time people couldn't even decide their own death. Can you imagine?"

"Don't say *death*," Gemm chided her gently. "It's harsh."

"All right. Recycle. Wouldn't you hate not being able to choose? Just yesterday Mori and Mora told me they intend to go next week."

A kind of chill gripped Gemm, like iron hands clasping his shoulders, moving around to his heart. "Mori? Mora? You mean, they want to . . . leave? Why?"

Gemma pulled away from Gemm's grasp. "What's the matter with you? Maybe they're bored. They don't feel like parenting, they haven't found a career they like, and anyway, it's their right to recycle anytime they want."

"But . . . but . . . don't you care? I thought you liked them."

"Of course I like Mori and Mora, but there are plenty of others— what's the matter with you, Gemm? Why do you care if they choose to recycle? It's their right!"

A sense of emptiness suddenly overwhelmed Gemm 16884, and all he could think of to describe it was the feeling he had had once, years ago, when the Meal Mate was empty and it took hours for it to be repaired. Gemma had run to get the Leader, who immediately summoned help. Now his breathing felt erratic, and his voice was strange even in his own ears. "I'll miss them," he said. "I . . . I wish—"

"Wishes are wasteful," Gemma recited.

Suddenly Gemm had a vision of all the people he had ever known, filing past him in identical gait, wearing identical jumpers except for color—all wearing faces that were somehow alike even though the designers tried to make them amusing and interesting. There seemed to be a huge gap somewhere, preventing him from seeing and knowing, though what it was he lacked he could not begin to say.

"Gemma," he whispered, and there was a terrible urgency in him, a sense that if he did not seize this moment, something vital would be lost forever. "Gemma, let me look at you."

"I'm here," she said, her voice muffled. "Go to sleep, my twin."

"I mean—I want—I need . . ." Almost of their own volition, Gemm's fingertips traced the flesh of Gemma's cheek, the line of her jaw, and Gemm's breath caught in his chest and throat as his trembling fingers pulled at the edge of her mask.

"What are you doing?" Gemma cried in alarm. "Gemm 16884, are you utterly *flashed*?"

"Please," Gemm whispered, his mind grasping for the right words to express his longing. "Let me, I beg you, just look upon your face. Remove your mask. Just for a moment, let me see—"

Gemm felt the bed careening under him as Gemma flipped the switch.

In the next moment, Gemma fled along the hallway and vanished from Gemm's sight.

CHAPTER
THREE

Gemm 16884 had never before run out into the night alone. He knew Gemma would be with Kira or Zoa or other friends. Perhaps because she was female, life was easier for her. She did not form strange attachments. Ever since childhood he had felt different. He would form an attachment to a certain toy, a particular playmate. He knew that these aberrations had been noted in his file. At his evaluation when he was eight, he had been promised by the Leader that he would outgrow them. And he had tried, locking in on his lessons, memorizing the wisdom that was provided for everyone on the screen.

Now, as he ran from the compound after flashing his wristband at the screen, Gemm 16884 felt a terrible, oppressive fear. He was *different*. The word haunted him. He ran far over the turf, toward the artificial red-rock mountains, almost as if he were living out his dream. Different and deviant. *Flashed*. His own twin had fled in disgust. Perhaps, like Mori and Mora, he ought simply to choose recycling and end it all. The thought stunned him.

He had, of course, been present at many recyclings of the old. He had watched the process with wonder and amazement. It began with a five senses Joy Drome presentation that was said to be quite beyond anything one usually experienced, reserved only for those about to be recycled. Of course, the onlookers did not share in the experience, but they saw the expressions of bliss on the faces of those who were leaving, and heard their cries of joy.

And yet, each time Gemm had witnessed a recycling, he had felt this same sorrow, like a void in his heart. To leave! Never to see the stars again, either in nature or in synthesis. Never to lie beside one's twin again, to talk, to browse and breathe and belong! No. He wanted to experience his full quota of 120 years. Then, the recycling would come as a natural and universal event. Besides, it wasn't fair to Gemma. If he recycled, it would leave her Single. Most Singles soon chose to join their recycled twins. Life alone was almost unbearable.

He knew how Gemma looked forward to the parenting, the parties and games, special foods, new clothes, and most of all, the gold. She talked a great deal about uncertainty, but it was just talk—mostly fem-talk. All the girls in their birth batch were preoccupied with it; and all of them, no matter how much they protested, would end up parenting, if not this year, then the next. If he left Gemma now, she'd never have a chance.

Gemm began slowly to climb the artificial red-rock mountain, feeling the lightness that always accompanied real exercise. In the dark, his bare feet found the footholds, his hands grasped the ledges and pillars with which he pulled himself up to the very top. As he reached the highest level, he spread out his arms, threw back his head, and felt the soft night air surrounding him and saw the stars looking down. He took a deep breath, filling his chest with air. He opened his mouth and let it happen. Oh! Oh! Melody. Song. Rhythm. All the things he had learned about only in ironic and amusing Folk Facts now seemed to rush upon him, the name of it combining with the feelings. *Music.* It was music that stirred within him, music he had to release—had to, or die! Arms akimbo, legs spread, Gemm stood at the top of the red-rock mountain and sang out, unthinking, uncaring, as if there were a gap in the universe and he was filling it with his song.

"Come along," said a voice, benign and mechanical. "Time to come along with us, there's a good fellow."

Just below him stood four transporters, lit from behind so that their red-and-black jumpers and their stark-white numbers blazed out at Gemm. "Come along. There's a good fellow."

"No! I'll jump!"

"It is forbidden to do violence to your body. You know it. Come. Nobody will hurt you."

"I'm not afraid of pain!"

"The only pain is from disharmony. Come along. Conformity begets Harmony begets Tranquillity . . ."

Gemm felt a sting on the side of his cheek. The beam had pierced his mask, causing a numbness to spread over his entire face, then down to his body. With the numbness came drowsiness and a floating feeling, and his thoughts drifted unsubstantially, pleasantly to waves of color vibrating all around him.

He was borne on a litter to the conveyor, still drifting and dreaming, lapsing into deep darkness and long, long sleep.

Words fluttered into his sleep state, sounds that became rhythms, rhythms that became songs. In his sleep, Gemm 16884 sang and danced. In his dreams now, Gemm 16884 lived only for music.

Voices awakened him. Gemm stirred and opened his eyes. A shaft of light beamed into his eyes. The medic stood over him with a laser probe. Med Com was attached to his arms. He became aware of a faint rhythmic sound: *Umpa, pumpa, humm, de-humm-da.* What was it? Ah, air being filtered into the vents, breezes; they made sounds, like music. *Umm, humm, pumpa, ummm.*

"Feeling better, Gemm 16884?"

"I feel . . . dazed." He noticed the earphones on the small table beside the bed. "How long have I been here?"

"Three days and nights," replied the medic. "All the while with sleep-teaching, as you can see." The medic drew back. "Get up," he said. "Walk."

Gemm 16884 obeyed. He swung his legs over the side of the bed and stood up. Then, carefully lifting one foot after the other, he walked, trying to look normal. But the sounds possessed him—*umpa pumpa, hum dee*—making him swing his arms and thrust out his legs in rhythm.

"Farther," said the medic, shaking his head. "Have you always walked this way?"

"What way?"

"Like . . . like a boat. Sailing on water. You know. Rising and falling. Not like . . . like the rest of us." The medic tilted his head, watching. He punched several keys, then reached for the printout, read it swiftly, and said, "It says here that when you were eight years old it was already noted. An odd gait. Didn't they tell you?"

"I don't remember." Gemm shook his head, trying to shake away the rhythm and the melody that was building now, brimming over in his mind: *Umpa, pumpa, hum, dee.*

"Of course," the medic said, "one would wish to forget such a thing as . . . deviance, wouldn't one?" The medic's tone had taken on a sharp edge. "And were you also making those noises? What do they call it, *music? Songs?* In Past Time, they say, people used to indulge in all kinds of movements and outcries. They even did it for one another, and they screamed and leaped about and did disgusting things with their bodies."

"Like this?" cried Gemm. He began to laugh, and he whirled and spun around, singing, singing to the beat, *"Umpa, pumpa, hum, dee!"* He clasped the medic's hand. "Try it! It's wonderful! Why won't you even try it? Do it! It's wonderful. *Hum, dee . . . la, la!"*

Astounded, the medic shook himself free and reached for the panel behind him, summoning help. But Gemm, though he noticed, didn't stop, couldn't stop. He was singing!

"Obviously," said the medic, sighing heavily, "the sleep sessions did not help. You are quite ill, Gemm 16884. Come. Rest." He caught Gemm by the arm and led him over to the bed. "How long have you been having these flashes? These dreams? You must have had them for quite some time. Isn't it so? You must tell me, Gemm 16884. These outbursts are dangerous both to you and to others. Tell me."

"I . . . don't know. Maybe always."

"You must know. It is perverse to keep secrets." The medic clasped Gemm's arms. "In love, I beg you to let me help you!"

Gemm saw the medic's eyes, outlined by the mask, gazing into his eyes with an intensity that frightened him back to reality.

"A long time," Gemm admitted. "As a small child, I used to . . . to . . . want to . . ." He felt his face burning. No, he could not say it. Would not. But the medic pressed his face close to Gemm's and placed his hands on Gemm's chest in a strange, oppressive touch.

"I wanted to be kissed."

"Kissed?" The medic's tone revealed his struggle. "By whom?"

"Anyone. My teachers. My . . . twin."

"But of course she did not engage in—"

"No, no. Never. I swear it!"

"Passion begets evil," the medic recited sternly. "Emotion undermines tranquillity. You know that such feelings are forbidden."

"I know it." A coldness had crept into the medic's eyes. Gemm shuddered. "Can't you give me something? Some kind of further instruction?" Gemm squirmed on the bed, trying to raise himself up. "I . . . I think I'm feeling better now. In love, I ask forgiveness."

"That won't do," the medic said calmly. Shadows formed as two other medics came to join the first one. They also wore the whites of their profession. One wore a gray mask; the other's was pale blue.

"We need transport here, I think," said the first medic. "Check him out. See if you agree. The bodily signs are erratic. Hormone level severely elevated. He's been suffering from frequent flashes resulting in aggressive behavior and . . . deviance."

The last word seemed to echo in the room.

"What about retraining? Sleep-teaching?"

"Negative results. We've had him wired up for three days."

One of the medics scratched his neck. "Looks like a recycle candidate."

"I concur."

Suddenly Gemm felt his arms being strapped down tight, and a weight, like a sheet of metal, coming down over his chest. He cried out and tried to move, but the straps held him immobile. "Wait! Wait!" he screamed. "You have no power, no right . . . I have choices!"

"When three agree," intoned the medics in unison, "when three agree, the deed is done."

"No! I ask—I demand to see my twin!" cried Gemm.

"Granted," said the first medic, his eyes piercing and hard. "You may talk to her. But it will change nothing."

. . .

They had dressed him in a beautiful, soft, white jumper, both cool and pleasantly warm. The fabric generated its own fragrance, a light floral scent. Still, Gemm was not soothed.

"It is the nature of your illness," the medic told Gemm when he complained of the lingering stress. "Sometimes even the best medications fail. It is a matter of—well, a predisposition to . . . a congenital aberration."

"If it is congenital," Gemm argued, "wouldn't my twin have it, too? We are perfectly matched genetically, except for our sex, of course. And what about my donors? Surely there are people like me, relatives—"

"Relatives!" the medic said, aghast. "Where do you get such notions? As in Past Time, when people lived in families? We have long outgrown such things. Besides, everything is not genetically determined. Look, all will be explained to you by a Leader, as is required by law. Your twin will be present, and any friends that you and she request. Everything will be according to form," the medic assured him. The medic moved toward the door, then turned back and said, "There's nothing to fear. Recycling is a most exhilarating experience. They say it is the zenith of feeling."

Gemm did not reply. Anything he said now could be used against him, further proof of his deviance. He lay back, trying to remember bits of information that had come to him from others—rumors, ideas, and thoughts. All night he had lain awake trying to remember, but he could not. All he knew was that a Leader would come to formally announce it. His file would be stamped, and he would go in the red-and-black transport to the recycle chamber and never come back.

Gemm 16884 went to the window, but its opaqueness mocked him. Never to see the trees again, or the stars, or the sky! He thought of all the things he had yet to experience with Gemma and their friends. They had talked of flying to the wilderness, seeing the Past Time ruins and bones of extinct animals and ancient structures. They had planned to take the galaxy mission, to visit the outer seas, to track the planets and leap into spaces on the moon. There were a thousand games to be played, puzzles to decipher, people to know, foods to taste, programs to test. How could he leave it all behind?

Gemm heard footsteps. He ran to the door but could see nothing except his own hazy reflection. All in white, except for his mask, he looked unreal, as if he were already recycled into vapor and dust.

The door lifted and Gemma rushed in, her hands reaching toward him.

"Gemm 16884!" she cried out.

"Gemma! Did you bring others?"

"No." She shuddered. "They all—" Her voice broke. "They shun me."

"Oh, no. Kir and Kira? Zo and Zoa? Everyone?"

She nodded, her face down in her hands. "Only Mori and Mora will sit with me and talk to me. It doesn't matter to them. They are recycling anyhow. Oh, Gemm, I've been so lonely. If you leave, I'm going with you. I can't bear it alone!"

The door lifted. First Gemm saw the gold jumper, then the numbers 77520, and the two entered, male and female. Leader 77520 strode forward. His twin followed, nodding to Gemma.

"Tranquillity," Leader 77520 greeted Gemm. He nodded to his twin. "This is Fem 77520. Our informal names are Eti and Eta. You may use our familiar names, under the circumstances."

"Thank you," whispered Gemma, her hands clasped under her chin. She wore a mask of pale lavender, making her look docile and somehow shrunken.

"We have come to prepare you and to inform you," said Eti.

"It is the law," added his twin.

"In love, we present you with choices."

"Choices?" repeated Gemm. "What choices?"

"A thousand choices," said Eta calmly. "Before recycling, you can choose your meal, your garments, colors, whispers, screens—everything will be as you wish it. You will recycle in bliss."

Gemma broke in. "Isn't there another choice?"

Silence followed, broken only by the hum of the screen. "There are always choices," said Leader 77520. "I was about to mention it." He glanced at his twin. "There is the possibility of petition."

Eta leaned toward Gemm. "Very few succeed."

"He must be given the opportunity," said Eti. "It is the law."

"What opportunity?" Gemm exclaimed. "I was told there is no cure for me."

"It would be up to the Elders," Eti said quietly. "And there would be decisions for you to make—deep decisions."

Eti 77520 sat down on a body mold and motioned his twin and Gemma to do likewise. "We will tell you. Nothing will be hidden from you." He tapped his knuckles together, took a deep breath, and continued. "You have perhaps seen the cluster of buildings far up on the mountains, across the three valleys. Maybe when you were on a hover trip you noticed."

"The palace?" Gemma asked. "All of glass and alabaster?"

"It is not a palace," said Eta with a slight laugh. "People call it that. It is really the heart, the center of—"

"That's enough, Eta," chided her twin. "They need only know about the part that concerns them now."

"In love, you are right," said Eta, ducking her head. "Those buildings contain, among other things, a clinic," she continued.

"Sometimes, in special cases," said Eti, "one who is found deviant may petition to be considered for The Cure. It is rare to be accepted. Rarer still to complete The Cure."

"But why is it so rare?" Gemm felt breathless. Now he remembered hearing rumors of strange happenings in the distant mountains, people vanishing or being transformed. Transformed into what? He and his friends had always thought this was a myth, something like a Folk Fact, maybe true, maybe only designed for amusement. This, then, was the idea that had nudged at his memory before but which he could not summon. *There was a cure.*

The two leaders shared a lingering, reluctant look. "For one thing," said Eti softly, "it involves pain."

"Pain," echoed his twin.

"For another," continued Eti, "few can withstand the procedure. When given the choice, most people choose swift and beautiful recycling. At least that is a known quantity. And painless."

Gemm 16884 gazed at his twin. Neither of them had ever experienced pain, only momentary intimations of it—a slight cut or cramp, healed almost immediately by a jetting of medication or a beam of the laser. Yet the thought of pain terrified Gemm, and he heard Gemma's swift breathing and saw the flickering in her eyes.

"Gemm," she said, moving toward him, "you need not experience pain. Don't do it for me. I will go with you, swiftly and sweetly. They say that the recycling is the most dazzling experience, quite amazing, quite—"

"In love," Gemm 16884 said loudly, "I will make this decision, not you. I will go into pain. I will petition. I will do anything to live."

CHAPTER FOUR

Gemma was not allowed to accompany him, though she begged the Leaders. "We have never been separated. Gemm, don't you want me?"

"Of course I do!" he exclaimed, reaching toward his twin.

"That's enough," said the Leaders. "We will not report this outburst of passion, because you are in an extreme state. Control yourself, Fem 16884. Find your friends. Have them take you to the Serotonin Bar."

"May I speak with my twin?" Gemma whispered. Her shoulders were hunched, her head down.

"For a moment," said Eta sternly.

Gemma whispered into Gemm's ear. "Be careful, my twin. I spoke to Mori and Mora. They were taken to the clinic and offered terrible choices. Mora refused them. You can do the same."

"You said they chose to recycle because they were bored!" Gemm exclaimed.

"Time," said Eti and Eta together.

"One moment more, I beg you!" Gemm pleaded. He turned to Gemma. "What did they tell you?"

"Mora was discovered to be . . . deviant. I'm not sure how. They said she was a danger to society. They took her to this clinic and they gave her a choice, but it was so ugly that she chose to recycle."

"Come along now," said the Leaders, each grasping one of Gemm's arms. "It is perverse to indulge like this in sentiment. You both know it!"

The two Leaders sat beside Gemm on the transport, which hovered for a few moments, then lifted. As the transport left the ground, Gemm was seized with profound loneliness. He looked down upon his compound, the turf, the artificial red-rock mountains, the spots of color that were the jumpers of his friends. He might never see any of this again. He could not understand those who chose to recycle. Not at all. It was, he thought with a heavy feeling, part of his deviance. Most people did not cling so passionately to life as he did.

After a time Gemm looked out and saw the rose-colored shapes of many buildings, seemingly attached but obviously mobile.

The transporter hatch swung open. "Alight," said Eti.

"Aren't you coming with me?" Gemm asked. The air seemed to have been altered; he could hardly breathe.

"No," Eta said. "One must be summoned."

"I have been summoned?"

"Your petition was answered. It is a summons. Go," Eti said sternly.

"What will happen to my twin?" Gemm asked. He gazed up at the alabaster building, at the great door, which he now saw was made of solid steel, although it looked pearly white.

"If you are not cured," Eta said, "she can choose to recycle with you."

"What if I am cured? Will everything be as before?"

"Time enough to discuss these things later," said Eti brusquely.

"I want to know!" Gemm 16884 cried. "It is perverse to keep secrets!" But the transport lifted and in the next moment was gone. Gemm stood alone. The landscape was utterly barren, a great desert devoid of any rocks—either real or artificial—trees, plants, birds, or any life-form. Coarse sand lay as far as the eye could see, flat and inhospitable.

The door swung open. Before him loomed a large tube set into a high-vaulted space like a cave. It was dark. Gemm stood there—how long he could not say—but after a time he could make out the edges of the tube and a faint blue light in the distance. He stood motionless, hearing his own breathing. Terror gripped him. The walls seemed to move in upon him. He lifted his head. His mind fastened on a single phrase: *Shout praises! Shout praises!* What could he possibly praise? He searched his mind. He was alive. He still had choices. *Shout praises!* his inner voice called.

Air currents rushing past indicated that he was moving—up or down, he could not tell—but the speed made Gemm close his eyes and brace himself, hands on his knees, head down. Things suddenly slowed. Gemm felt himself being lifted up ever so slightly, then set down, like a petal in the wind. He looked up. The tube was filled with light. Voices urged him to move forward, until he stood at another door that glowed green and seemed to vibrate with energy.

"Scanner," requested an unseen voice.

Gemm held up his wrist as directed. The vibrating light intensified. "We have expected you," said the voice. "Follow the path, please."

Another door opened, then another and another, and Gemm 16884 moved along, his heart beating so wildly that all thoughts of control vanished. He was caught, like a creature in a 3-D maze, like a twig inside a flame. Breezes and whispers urged him along until he stood in a large room circumvented by translucent walls, through which Gemm barely glimpsed rows of stadium seats.

Spectators filled half a dozen of the seats. Gemm 16884 could see nothing more than their shapes and their cloaks of deep blue velvet. It was the sacred color and fabric used only by Elders. Their masks were of woven gold, so that their faces shone. Gemm had never seen an Elder up close, but he had seen their images on the screen, of course; and once, from a distance, he saw several of them walking together.

Nobody Gemm knew had ever gazed upon an Elder or spoken to an Elder, or even contemplated doing so. Now his limbs felt oddly numb as a voice called to him, stern and echoing in the large chamber. "Step into the form, please!"

Gemm 16884 turned and saw to his astonishment that the translucent walls had been transformed into a hologram of brilliant colors. A human shape was outlined there. Gemm stepped into the mold, spreading his arms and legs to accommodate the shape. Instantly the hologram changed. Brilliant colors and shapes alternated; the screens broke into several images.

A loud, resonant voice filled the air. "Step away now, please."

As Gemm stepped to the center of the room, a person moved toward him through the hologram. Gemm stared at the blue velvet cloak, the gold mask, and the gold-leaf numbers emblazoned at the Elder's throat. The Elder seemed to float on air, nodding as he went. "Conformity begets Harmony," said the Elder. His words seemed to hang in the air, like bright objects.

Gemm 16884 lowered his eyes to the floor and bent his head in reverence. He responded softly, his voice quaking, "Harmony begets Tranquillity."

"But not for you," the Elder said sternly. "You are not tranquil. However, you have courage, Gemm 16884."

"In love," said Gemm humbly, "I thank you." He felt dizzy from confusion. Some said that Elders were not really human. It was rumored that they could fly, that they could resurrect dead things, that they could raise a person up and transport him by the sheer force of their will.

"Oh, don't thank me," said the Elder. "You may have reason yet to curse me!"

"Never," gasped Gemm. Surely the Elder was joking. But did Elders make jokes? He had no idea.

"This hologram," said the Elder, "shows various genetic models and brain structures." Indeed, while they were speaking, the hologram changed continually into new patterns and sequences. "Your genetic structure is being coded and analyzed. Almost ready. There it is. And your file. Up-to-date, to the microsecond."

A portion of the wall drew back, revealing the seated Elders, all of whom now faced Gemm. He blinked at the sight of their glowing masks, and his breath caught in his throat. Nobody would ask why he was here. Nobody would inquire as to his crime. They already knew. Not only his genetic code but his entire life—every infraction, every merit, every major choice—was imprinted here. Gemm 16884 shuddered. There was no place to hide.

The Elder strode up to Gemm, and with his hands clasped behind his back, he proclaimed, "Gemm 16884, you have been diagnosed as deviant. Every possible attempt has been made to rehabilitate you to no avail. You are a criminal, Gemm 16884—aggressive, hostile, nonconforming. We have noted tendencies toward *diversity* in your gait, in your dreams, and most especially in your repeated persistence in"—the Elder cleared his throat—"making music."

The chamber was silent, except for the faint clicking of the hologram as it proceeded through its sequences.

The Elder stood silent for a moment, then continued. "It is clear from your readout that certain random processes were at work during your brain's development, processes that no amount of genetic engineering could control. A person's genetic makeup provides only a blueprint. Sometimes random variations do creep in. When this happens, when we fail, our failures must be recycled. It is unfortunate but nothing personal. You understand, I'm sure."

Gemm nodded. It was difficult to grasp that the Elder was talking to him, about him, for the encounter seemed so distant. "What happened?" Gemm asked in a hushed, strange tone. "What is wrong with my brain to make me so deviant?"

"In your case," said the Elder, nodding toward the hologram, "it looks as if the cerebellum—that part of the brain that is receptive to rhythm and tone—is too highly developed. Once, all humans had such developed cerebellums; and these created countless problems. Our genetic engineers have been able to shrink the cerebellum to a more acceptable level. You, however, are—well, what one might call a throwback. We don't know why. Perhaps something happened in the Womb Room, or perhaps you were dropped as an infant and thus developed new connections that created this enlargement. It's difficult to know."

"Can you cut out this . . . this large cerebellum?" Gemm 16884 asked. "Can you cause it to shrink?"

"No," said the Elder. "There is only one possibility for a cure, if you are willing to undertake it."

"I will do anything!" Gemm called out. His outburst was met with grim silence. Obviously this passion, too, was considered part of his illness.

The Elder drew back. He was not finished with his sermon and continued now, facing both Gemm and his audience, which had, in the interim, grown to several dozen persons, all wearing the deep blue velvet and the gold.

"Gemm 16884," declared the Elder, "it is established with us for all time that uncontrolled behavior is dangerous, not only to the individual, but to the entire social order. In Past Time, there was a period when people lauded diversity. Yes, they actually encouraged it. People *wanted* to be different."

Embarrassed laughter rippled out and was quickly dispelled, and the Elder continued loudly, "Yes, they craved differences in their dress, their looks, their possessions. As one might expect, this led to fierce competition and strife—even to killing, even to wars. Oh, yes!" the Elder called out as a few murmurs escaped from the audience. "You may wonder, how does music fit in? In Past Time, people used to create what they called songs praising a certain individual for his differences. I tell you this because you are all mature and can process such information without letting it upset you unduly. People used to select their own mates—a special specific person, whom one then *loved* for his or her individuality."

Murmurs of disbelief came from the spectators.

"Furthermore," shouted the Elder, his hands lifted briefly for attention, "people created music and poetry and stories out of the very notion that they *were* different, that they had the right to express their own ideas. They thought they could change the world, *improve* the world, not with genetics and drugs and therapy as we now employ, but with . . . with those deviant behaviors they called arts and creativity and dialogue. It went on and on, this absurdity."

The Elder allowed his audience a moment to comprehend these astonishing facts. Then he lifted both hands again, and raised his voice to a shout. "We now know the truth. Diversity results not in universal good but in evil. We know that music, art, dance, poetry—all these ancient and deviant activities—only inflame the emotions. They must be rooted out. We discovered long ago that there is but one road to Universal Good, and that road begins with Conformity."

Now the spectators began to chant in unison, and Gemm added his voice to theirs.

"Conformity begets Harmony begets Tranquillity begets Peace begets Universal Good. Shout praises!"

The Elder now placed his two hands on Gemm's shoulders and looked deep into Gemm's eyes. "Gemm 16884, I have one question to ask you. Do you sincerely wish to conform?"

"In love, I sincerely do," replied Gemm 16884. He felt near weeping, but he breathed deep, seeking self-control.

"Then there is but one possibility for you. The Cure is painful. It is uncertain of success. It will lead you into realms you cannot imagine, have never experienced, and will not be able to share with anyone."

"What is The Cure?" Gemm whispered.

The Elder took a solemn stance, hands locked behind his back, head raised to the audience of Elders, who listened in awe. "Gemm 16884, from Past Time we have an extensive record of events that actually occurred. They are called History. These records are used only in extreme cases such as yours. Now, we can take from this History a certain event, appropriate to your condition. We can cause you to experience this event so as, we hope, to effect a cure."

Gemm gazed past the Elder to the hologram, where his entire inner structure was starkly revealed. He asked, "How can one experience Past Time?"

The Elder said, "The event will be downloaded directly into your brain, a program complete in every detail—physical, mental, and emotional. You will experience this event quite as if you were really there. In other words, Gemm 16884, you will become another person, living in Past Time, experiencing that person's growth and pain. Any more questions?"

Gemm floundered for a moment in confusion, then asked, "How will this cure me?"

"Simply put," replied the Elder, "we are shaped by our experiences. This experience will, if we are successful, completely erase your deviant desire to make music. Music—that road to emotion, to passion, to deviance—will be erased from your mind. The very thought of music will be totally repugnant to you. You will be, in other words, perfectly adapted. Cured." The Elder stood back for a long moment, nodding, giving Gemm a piercing look. The glow from the Elder's mask seemed to strike Gemm between the eyes, almost blinding him.

"Now you have been given warning and choice," said the Elder. "What is your reply?"

"I am ready," said Gemm.

Strapped onto the table, Gemm lay motionless. He could see everything through various monitors, and he knew that countless others also observed the procedure and his reactions. What did it matter? He was like an object, transparent and without feelings, something to be prodded, analyzed, perhaps later discarded. All this Gemm 16884 accepted. But even as he listened to the explanations, he heard the faint and beautiful strains of song, far in the distant atmosphere and near, deep within his own being. Thus divided, he was able to endure the terror.

Special technicians appeared. Gemm felt their fingertips upon his head and his body. He heard the scanners humming.

As the procedure took place, the Elder continually explained. "We are implanting the electrodes in your brain now, into the posterior hypothalamus called the raphe. This is the seat of neuron transmitters that produce serotonin. As you know, serotonin promotes tranquillity. This chemical will now be partially blocked. Another electrode is being introduced into the tegmentum of the midbrain. This will heighten sensations of pain or pleasure. Another in the hypothalamus will produce histamines to stimulate the entire system and create excitement, especially sexual arousal."

Gemm glimpsed the tiny electrodes, the various devices being loaded into his brain, and he felt no pain. Obviously the drug they had injected into his body was already working.

Occasionally he felt an odd sensation, not unpleasant, as the probes continued. "See here," the Elder was saying, "it is evident on the scan: the enlargement of the cerebellum. This is the source of his problems. As I already explained, the cerebellum regulates

balance and rhythm. This grotesque overdevelopment causes our subject, here, to be attracted to such things as rhythm and tone—in other words, the components of music."

"And does this also account for that strange walk of his?"

Gemm 16884 heard light laughter. "Yes. I wouldn't be surprised if he were also inclined to dance."

There was a short, shocked silence.

"In love, permit me, please, to ask one question more," asked a technician.

"Yes? Yes?"

"How is the past incident selected? It seems that a whole host of incidents might be applicable."

"Well, now, we have experts for this. Our master biologist-historians are qualified to make the proper selection, depending on the circumstances. In this case, because the subject expresses his deviance with music, we selected an experience where music is prominent—and is associated with pain."

Gemm listened with a strange feeling of detachment.

"In a few moments now," murmured the Elder to Gemm, "you will be there. In Past Time. Think of it as an adventure."

"But—while I am there, in Past Time, will I know who I really am? Will I remember this present?" Gemm gazed at the ceiling with its colors and patterns; he breathed deeply the fragrant air. He could not imagine life in another time, without his friends or his twin.

The Elder paused, drawing a deep breath. "You will not remember," he said. "However, the absorption rate of the drugs you are receiving may vary. When that occurs, you may experience 'flashes' of this present life. Probably you will experience them as dreams or odd thoughts—the way you are experiencing the flashes of music now."

"I will not know that I am from the future," Gemm said sleepily.

"You will not know," acknowledged the Elder soberly.

"When will we know whether or not The Cure was effective?" Gemm asked.

"When you awaken, as from a dream."

"How long will I be away in Past Time?" Feebly Gemm tried to move. He could not. Something seemed to hold him down. His eyes felt heavy.

"For one full day," replied the Elder. "But it will seem like one year."

"If I am not myself, who will I be? Where will I go?"

The Elder drew near, gazing down into Gemm's eyes. "You will be living in the small city of Strasbourg in the land once named Germany, in the year 1348. You will be known as Johannes, son of Menachem the Jew."

"What is a Jew?" Gemm asked sleepily.

"You will discover it soon," promised the Elder.

CHAPTER
FIVE

There is frost still on the ground in early morning. Carts clatter by quickly; the horses blow white breath from their nostrils. People scurry through the narrow alleyways. The wind blasts women's skirts up around their ankles and blows men's caps away. In Cathedral Square the cobblestones are slick and treacherous. Townsfolk cluster there, eager to trade and perhaps to catch some news from a traveling peddler or a monk returned from Avignon. We are all hungry for news, just as we are hungry for green growing things.

It is spring again. A few daffodils are showing traces of yellow in certain secret spots: just beside the public bathhouse, down by the mill, and amid the short, stocky grapevines, which have been dormant all winter.

Somehow I never feel that I can play as well in winter, when the notes from my flute lie frozen against the walls of the house or suffocated in the heat from the blazing hearth. "Play something, Johannes," Grandmother says, already smiling to herself at the promise of music. I play the tunes that Oma loves, but their melancholy key soon makes everyone anxious and tired, and Father comes out from the alcove where he keeps his money boxes, clapping his large hands, calling, "Children! Enough now of play; to the books! The books!"

Carefully Father brings the great volume down from the shelf, almost cradling it against his chest, setting it down on the massive wooden table. He opens it slowly, as if its wisdom must not be exposed too quickly or carelessly to the world. "We read from the parasha . . . ," and he gives the name of the weekly reading. "Bereshit" or "Noah" or "Lech Lecha," whichever it is. Always stories are woven in between the text, sometimes laughter, too, as Grandfather tells of happenings when he was a boy in France, before the expulsion. Grandfather never forgets that he had to leave his beloved home, just because he was a Jew.

Now I lean against the stone wall of our house, holding my flute, waiting and hoping for an audience—not just any audience, but the two special sisters, Margarite and her little sister, Rosa, who is the same age as my sister, Rochele. Margarite is sixteen, like me.

All winter, Margarite's cheeks have been rosy from cold, and her thick red hair nearly hidden under a heavy black shawl. Her eyes are always the same, sparkling brown, with a certain kind of laughter in them. I do love to make Margarite laugh and tap her feet. Father and Mother say it is a gift from God, the way I make the music bounce and leap. Uncle David, laughing and rolling his eyes, says I could even set a rabbi to dancing at a funeral!

"Johannes, what in the world are you doing out there? Is there no work to be done for the Seder, that you can sit and dream?" Mother's voice is robust and full. She scolds, like all mothers, but then she soothes with a small pursing of her mouth, a hasty caress with the back of her hand. Besides, I have been running all day, getting wood for the fire, bringing in wine, bartering for candles and eggs and yet more eggs.

"I'm hungry!" I call, but it's only a game. No food until tonight— of course not! Haven't we hungered all day, with the smell of that scrawny chicken swelling in the soup pot, and fish and apples chopped so fine they will melt on the tongue! Beyond that, a good chunk of lamb is roasting on the spit, enough to make one faint. Ah, Seder is the best meal of the year, with wine for everyone, even the children. Twelve-year-old Benjamin and little Rochele drink their wine mixed with a good deal of water. For the past two years I have drunk it pure—pure heaven, heady and sweet. We will sing and sway in our chairs, reclining as is the custom at the Seder.

Grandmother sits by the fire, cracking more nuts for the *harosis*. She complains that, with her few teeth, she cannot chew, but always she puts more and more nuts into the apple mixture, defying nature, it seems. It is a rare thing to have two old people in the house. Grandmother and Grandfather sleep in the small chamber off the main room. Everyone else sleeps upstairs. We are lucky to have this house. Grandfather bought it many years ago, when Jews could still own property.

Suddenly Grandmother calls out sharply, frightened, "Where are the children? Where are the children?"

Mother turns away from her cooking and rushes to her side. "Didn't you send them out for water?"

"That was long ago, Miriam! It is nearly time for the Angelus. Where are they?"

Mother comes out and taps my arm. "Have you seen the children, Johannes?" Benjamin and Rochele are "the children." I am counted as an adult, already in business with my father and known by the gentiles as Johannes, son of Menachem, the moneylender. All my life I will be called Johannes, the moneylender—never Johannes, the musician, though I know in my heart that I am a musician.

I call back to Mother, "Don't worry. The sun is still at midpoint. They are only playing on the bridge, maybe picking frogs from the water, who knows?" I blow several notes on my flute to show my lack of concern. Mother vanishes into the house, and I can smell wood smoke and food scents in the air.

The sisters are not coming. Margarite is no doubt home, helping to prepare the Seder meal. Her father, Elias, is a sad-eyed man with red hair and a quiet disposition. Elias must endure the hatred of the gentile butchers who, when they see him, always spit.

"Johannes!" Grandmother calls, her tone crusty and irritable. "Go find the children. *Rasch! Rasch!* They should not be out so late on this day."

I go inside, where Grandmother sits and jerks the thread from her spindle. When I touch her fingertips, I feel them hardened forever from spinning. Mother is bringing spoons and bowls to the table. Tonight I will sit at the left hand of Father. He has said I will read part of the service. I am so eager for tonight to come.

"I'm going now, Oma." With my hand on Grandmother's back, I

can feel the sharp shoulder blades and the small hump on her back, even through her heavy shawl.

I put away my flute in its velvet case, take my hat and cloak. Mother calls after me, "Johannes! Bring me six more eggs from Frau Rivka, and take her this jar of honey."

She gives me a small net sack, lined with straw, for the precious eggs. We used to have some hens, but they were wont to die from disease or by malicious dogs; so now we trade honey for eggs, money for chicken.

I walk along the curved, narrow street. There is the hovel of Moshe the Bent. He used to weave with those fine, long fingers of his, until Jews were forbidden in the trades. Moshe has an old fiddle and plays it for weddings. Zemel, the baker, glances up from the oven inside his shop. He looks exhausted. He has baked *matzos* for all the Jews in Strasbourg, and his hands are swollen and burnt. He is not careless, only overworked. He is allowed only two apprentices and must pay a heavy tax for each. Such things are well regulated by the town council; one Jew baker, one butcher, one rabbi, three teachers, two tailors, and as many moneylenders as possible—let them kill one another with their competition.

From his upstairs loft, Dovie, the shipbuilder, long without work, calls out, "Hullo, Johannes! Watch yourself. Holy week starts tomorrow, but one never knows . . ."

I shrug and grin. "I know, I know."

The smell of herbs rises from Saul's garden. Even some gentiles buy from him, ignoring the law. Saul's hut is so small that in summer his children sleep on the roof. Last year one fell off to his death, and Saul's wife still weeps.

There is Rabbi Meier with his sons, standing at the upstairs window, nodding and waving. *"Gut yom tov!"* they shout, and I call back the same.

Nearer the cathedral are the grand houses of several wealthy Jews, like Vivelin Rote, who boasts that he lent sixty-one thousand florin to King Edward III of England. He and Jeckelin, another wealthy moneylender, dress in fur-trimmed cloaks. The villa on the corner belongs to Meister Jakon, the singer, whose fortune was inherited from his grandparents. The Jews grin when they see him and tell each other, "If I had his loot, believe me, I'd be singing, too!" Meister Jakon and I have played music together. Jakon's voice and my flute, people said, were like an angel choir.

At the canal I look for Benjamin and Rochele, calling their names. Rochele likes to tarry at the well and talk to people. Mama has told her a thousand times not to talk to strangers, but still she does. Benjamin is little better for sending on errands. He stops at every bridge, poking the water for frogs or fishes.

But the children are not at the canal. A sudden wind whips around between the tall brick watchtowers. Behind the towers is the forest, dense with trees and hidden animals. Once a family of wolves wandered right into the cemetery, staring, their tongues hanging out. Then peacefully they retreated. The local priests claimed it was a sign from Heaven, though what sort of sign, nobody knew, as nothing changed. Benjamin and Rochele would not venture into the forest, would they? They have heard stories of children disappearing there, and Rochele is desperately afraid of wolves.

I run over the low wooden bridge, feeling like a child again. I can smell the raw stench of hides laid out to dry. Beside the tanner's section are the butchers. Entrails and tufts of animal hair float in the gutter. At last I reach the square. But the honey still sits in the net sack. I have forgotten the eggs. Well, on the way home, then.

In the square, merchants are sweeping, closing up their stalls, dumping out filthy water buckets, kicking aside the horse dung and mud. Children run and shriek, and their mothers scream at them, "Stop it! No more wild play!" but they go on screaming and laughing as if they would never grow up to know the troubles of the world.

A small crowd is gathered across from the cathedral, listening to the ravings of a wandering friar. He wears a corded belt around his loose-woven linen tunic, which was once white but is now various shades of gray and tan. His beard is ragged, hanging halfway down his chest; his hair is wild. There, too, are Rochele and Benjamin, pushing against the crowd. I grab Benjamin by the shoulder and Rochele by the arm. They have set down the water bucket—bad children!—and are all ears and eyes. The friar is shouting, "Now you must know what happens to sinners!"

"Come away from here!" I scold, but Benjamin pushes my hand away.

"Come home. Mama is waiting. Oma is frantic. You don't belong here with all these people." But, in truth, I am also drawn in by the friar's ravings.

"Upon my soul, it happened just last autumn that a ship rode into the harbor at Messina, the main port in Sicily, and all its crew lay dead at the oars or dying. They had boils upon their flesh, under the armpits, and in the groin. Horrible black boils, they were, oozing pus and blood; and they spat blood and they stank of their poisonous pestilence—and after five days, all of them were dead."

Rochele gasps. Benjamin asks me, "Where is Sicily?"

"How would I know?"

"It is a pestilence sent by God, punishment for man's lust and greed. Repent now, ye sinners! Repent!"

"Aye," murmur several women, nodding, their hands folded over their breasts. "It is surely a sign from our Lord. Just last week Pastor Richards found a bloodstain on the altar cloth." They murmur and cross themselves.

The crowd draws back. Merchants return to their stalls. Rochele tugs at my arm. "What made those sailors die? Were they wicked, like Jonah? Did God punish them?"

"We know nothing," says Benjamin, "except that it is a strange pestilence."

"What sickness brings black boils?" Rochele asks. "And stinking?" She shudders. "Will it come to us, too?"

"No, no," I say, to soothe her. "The sickness—it is a sickness that comes to men at sea," I say, though in truth I know nothing of such plagues.

"Not only sailors die," Benjamin says darkly.

"Frau Rivka's babies both died," Rochele says. "In our family," she asserts, "children don't die. It is because of Grandmother's blessings over us."

"Hush!" I shout. "You do not say such things, ever."

"Thou must not tempt the devil," quotes Benjamin, "by saying how well thou art."

I pull them along. "Come, we must hurry." We go across the square, past the enormous bishop's palace, to the street of inns and fine stores and the homes of the wealthy burghers.

The guild house, with its sober facade and deep carvings, is decked with a satin banner of purple and gold. Beside it the tavern, or *trinkhaus,* emits the happy sounds of leisure and pleasure. Two men stumble out, arm in arm. The one with the red face is Betscholt, the butcher. The other is the Baron Zorn. The butcher teeters to one side, pointing at me. "It's that Jew child," he says. "Will they ever stop whelping these little moneylenders?" He laughs, showing brown-stained teeth.

I murmur to the children, "Run home. Leave the water, just run!" Benjamin and Rochele slip away, moving like shadows.

The men stagger toward me. I taste my own hatred on my tongue, but I feel frozen, unable to speak. Baron Zorn is powerfully built, and dressed in velvet leggings and a cloak with an ermine collar. He carries a walking stick inlaid with ivory. "Jews," he says, with spittle showing in the corners of his mouth, "what are you doing here? Isn't this your blood night?"

"Perhaps he comes to spy on us, Claus," says the butcher, Betscholt. "They hate us, you know. They only want to see us all perish."

I feel numb. I know this butcher and his son, Konrad. Konrad the Snake, they call him.

Baron Zorn proceeds. "Answer me!" he shouts. "You! Son of Menachem, the moneylender, don't you know that you will all rot in hell?" The two block my path, their postures menacing. Several merchants and children gather, waiting for the fun.

If they had not been drinking, these men would not even look at me. To them, I am less than a beetle in a pile of horse dung. But now—a gust of wind knocks my hat off. I lunge after it. The law says that all Jewish men must wear the dark pointed hat. Before I can reach the hat, the butcher, Betscholt, has placed his foot on it.

"Please, sir, my hat," I say. My heart knocks in my throat.

Betscholt steps back. I take the hat, replace it on my head.

Baron Zorn reaches out and, with his fist, knocks the hat off again, laughing. A second punch falls on my neck, leaving me gasping and stunned.

Laughter echoes as if it were rising from the cobblestones, bouncing off the walls.

I bend to pick up my hat again. I take up the water bucket, careful not to run. If I run, all will be lost.

"Devilish usurious rat!" someone screams.

"Come, children, don't look at him. You could go blind."

"They use the blood, you know, on this night."

The Angelus rings out. People scatter. It is time for late afternoon prayers, and the priests are waiting in their sanctuaries to teach them about sin.

"Good riddance!" a woman screams.

I clutch the bucket handle and the sack very tightly. At least they did not take the honey. I move my fingertips, pretending to be playing the flute, making music, but my legs are trembling, the breath is blocked in my throat, and in my heart there is no music.

Home at last, I give Mother the eggs. I feel perplexed, and I ask her, "Mother, is there truly a pestilence in the land, with people dying, with boils and pus?"

"Hush, hush," my mother soothes. "Where do you get such notions? Come wash your hands. It is nearly time for the festival."

Rochele's hair shines. She wears a new frock with a broad white collar and full, ruffled sleeves. Benjamin has new leather shoes. By tomorrow the shoes will look old, because Benjamin is like a wild horse.

Everyone is slicked and washed. The gentiles call all this washing craziness. They tap their heads when they see the Jews coming from the bathhouse.

Father rushes in, rubbing his hands together, eager to start. He has put his ledgers and money boxes away. He wears his white *kittel*, the linen garment in which he will someday be buried. He wears it on only one other day of the year, Yom Kippur. He and Mother exchange a glance, a smile. I find myself thinking of Margarite.

A knock at the door. Everyone starts. Grandfather grips the back of his chair. Rochele quickly squats down in her little place beside the hearth. The knock comes again, harder.

"I will go," says Father.

I go with my father, standing right behind him.

The heavy door swings open. The man outside is breathing hard, his belly bulging over his belt. He wears beautiful shoes, elaborately embossed, and a cap of maroon velvet.

Father opens the door wider. "Herr Zorn! Come inside; the wind is strong. Please, step in."

I know this man, the brother of my tormentor from the square.

Zorn shakes his head. "My business is brief," he says. "Also, I know it is the evening of your . . ." I can tell he does not want to say the word *Passover*. It repels him. He glances toward the table, hoping to see something that will justify his loathing. "I have only come for my pledge," he says firmly.

"Yes, well . . ." Father steps backward, stammering, for he has put his business aside already, in preparation for the holiday. Business is one thing, the soul is quite another, and tonight the spirit must prevail. "I shall get it for you straightaway," Father says.

As Herr Zorn steps inside, his gaze rests upon the table and the family assembled there.

Mother rushes forward. "Won't you sit down, Herr Zorn?"

"Thank you, no."

Grandmother plucks at the ends of her shawl. She averts her eyes from this man, as if by acknowledging his presence she would grant him even greater power.

I feel the man's weight in the room, as if he is taking up all the air. Suddenly I know exactly what will happen, as if it is already done. There can be only one outcome, especially on this night.

Father brings the ledger down from the wooden shelf, and the box with people's pledges inside—rings, necklaces, other treasures. He takes out the man's ring, heavy gold with a bright blue stone. I hear the snapping sound of the fire, the rumble of Grandfather's breath. Father opens his hand to show the ring lying there. Herr Zorn starts forward, snatches the ring, and places it on his middle finger. Father leaps back in alarm. "Herr Zorn," he says, "there is the further matter of repayment." He shows Zorn the ledger, its parchment pages filled with careful accounts.

Herr Zorn glances at the ledger. He laughs. "Ah, but that has been settled already, don't you know? Last month I sent my man to make partial payment. You were out. My man gave the money to your son. The rest is here." Zorn holds out a small handful of dull coins. "Surely you remember, Johannes? Didn't you write it down?"

I stare at the man, speechless; how dare I contradict him? My lips begin to tremble, also my hands. Cursed weakness! I clench my hands at my sides, making two fists.

"All repayments," says Father, "are recorded in this ledger. There must be some mistake, Herr Zorn."

Zorn draws himself up, his mouth puffed at the insult. "I do not make mistakes," he says. "You must teach your son to keep proper accounts. Or perhaps," the man says slyly, "he keeps his own little secret cache, eh?"

I feel as if my entire face has swelled up. To accuse a son of stealing from his father!

"I assure you, Herr Zorn," Father says, "my son is—"

"Perhaps he is only careless. Nevertheless," continues Zorn, "the law is very strict in these matters. My brother-in-law, the magistrate, will tell you. Last month he was resident at the castle and is soon to be appointed assessor for His Lordship."

The man's small eyes scan the room. "As you know, I consider myself your friend. Others, however, would not overlook such a breach, especially at this time of year. You know the accusations that are flying."

Herr Zorn looks once again toward the table. Everyone, even little Rochele, knows what he is looking for. From childhood the gentiles have heard it whispered in the lanes and shouted from the pulpit.

They have seen it in their nightmares. *On Passover night the Jews drink the blood of a Christian child to perform their service.* But where is the blood? Where?

Herr Zorn strides over to the table and slams down the few dull coins. Several of them roll onto the floor.

The man leaves. The chill remains. Silence holds everyone still as a stone. Silently I pick up the coins and put them away, and I feel dirty.

"How dare he come here!" I burst out.

Father gives me a meaningful look. He quotes, " 'Let my soul be silent to those who curse me.' Johannes, this is a special night, a beautiful night. Come to the table."

A thump at the door. This time the arrival is met with shouts of gladness; Uncle David is here, and he has brought his lute. Father looks out at the sky; it is still daylight. "Time for a quick song," says he, "before the holiday. Have you a tune, David?"

Between his full, curling dark beard, Uncle David's mouth makes a wide smile. "I have, indeed," says David. His dark eyes are merry; he is Mother's brother, with eyes like hers, wide-set cheekbones, and a kind mouth. "First a little dance," says David. As he strums the strings Mother's feet tap; she grasps Rochele by the hands and whirls her round and round. David gives me a wink and I run to get my flute. I play with him, adding high notes, trills, and a lovely harmony. It is a familiar tune, one that every child knows; but Uncle David embellishes it, so that it sings to the heart!

Then David says, "We must give thanks." And now, in a lovely voice, David sings the blessing, praising God for allowing us to reach this festive season.

I see Mother's face gleaming in the candlelight. The white kerchief wrapped around her hair emphasizes the brightness of her dark eyes and the blush on her cheeks. She is still so beautiful. But my father's face is a mystery. His eyes are heavy lidded, his lips taut as he glances my way. Can it be that deep down he harbors doubts about me? I try to smile, but I feel a slow anger within. I cannot seem to rid myself of it.

I try to clear my mind of Herr Zorn, heeding my father's admonition. It is a day to celebrate.

The pilgrimage play is always part of it. Benjamin, dressed as a pilgrim with a cardboard sword in one hand and a wooden staff in the other, comes lumbering in. His face is rubbed with coals to affect a beard. Rochele totters behind him, carrying a basket, playing the wife. Benjamin makes his voice deep. "Have ye lodging for pilgrims such as we?"

Father answers soberly, "Whence comest thou, O pilgrim?"

"From Egypt, where *Adonai* performed wonders for my people against the evil Pharaoh."

Rochele wears a white shawl wrapped around her head and shoulders. She is gleeful, clapping her hands. "We are free!" she shouts, as I have coached her.

"Whither goest thou?" asks Grandfather.

"To Jerusalem," reply Benjamin and Rochele together.

"Nay," says Father, "tarry with us awhile, to relive the story of the Passover and our escape from slavery."

Now come the stories of enslavement and eventual release, together with prayers of thanksgiving. Benjamin tries to sit still, but he squirms and laughs excitedly. He begs for full red wine, but Father still dilutes it.

Mother and Rochele bring in the soup. Father and Grandfather eat from one bowl, and Benjamin and Uncle David and I share another. Rochele, Grandmother, and Mother eat together at the end of the table. Their heads nearly touch over the blue gray bowl. They are all so calm, while my mind is racing.

I had a strange dream just before awakening this morning. It frightens me now to remember. In the dream nobody had a real face. They wore smooth masks of many different colors. How peculiar! Maybe it is a sign, but for what? I must ask Rabbi Meier. Dreams can be prophecies. In the dream, also, I stood on a strange mountain of red rock, odd and unfamiliar. What can it mean? Am I going to make a journey?

Nobody speaks as the savory soup, with its floating bits of chicken and carrot, goes down. Next comes the lamb. I carry it in on a deep wooden trencher, and with it, all the vegetables Mother could manage at this time of year; a squash or two, some corn and beans. Vegetables, eggs, fish, and meat all in one meal! *Matzos* for dipping in the bitter herbs and the sweet apple mixture, with some left over to go with the meat. Our fingers catch the drippings, spiced with pepper and precious salt. We lean back in our chairs, as is the custom, a symbol of freedom. Free men can lean; slaves must kneel or stand at attention.

During the stories and riddles, I find myself listening to the wind outside, tense from the portent of this week. How can Father sit here eating and smiling, after what Zorn has done? How can everyone eat so calmly, while I start at every sound? I must be a terrible coward, a weakling, always afraid, though I try not to show it.

When a knock comes at the door, Rochele turns pale. "Elijah," she whispers, overcome, for the prophet is said to appear at every Jewish home on Passover night to foretell the coming of *Moshiach,* the Messiah.

The door swings open. "Hullo! Am I late? Can I come in?"

I am overjoyed. "Jacob!"

Mother rushes to greet him. "Good God, it is Jacob, our dear young friend. Come in! Have you been long on the road? You look exhausted. You are still in time for supper—let all who are hungry come and eat!"

Jacob greets everyone in appropriate order. David rises and claps Jacob on the back. "Look at this young doctor!" he exclaims. "You left us as a boy, and now, look at his beard!" Jacob's dark whiskers are still sparse, but a beard, nevertheless.

Mother starts to fuss. "Quick, Rochele, bring a bowl and pitcher so that Jacob may wash."

"Here, sit beside me," says Father, making room.

Jacob and I grin at each other, then Jacob laughs as he squeezes my arms. "Are these the muscles of a money changer?" Jacob exclaims. "You must be hauling stones and lumber, eh? Rochele! You look like an angel. Benjamin, have you ridden any horses lately?"

It is like the old days, when Jacob and his parents were our neighbors, before Jacob went away to Paris to study medicine. Jacob's eyes reflect weariness and trouble, but he smiles at Grandmother and exclaims, "Ah, you have a new shawl for *yom tov*! May it get old, and may you have a new one!"

Mother lays her hand on Jacob's shoulder. "It is wonderful to see you, Jacob. Eat, then we will talk. You must be starved. Are you staying now in Strasbourg? Are you finished with school? We need someone like you here, God knows." She sighs, glances at Father, then brightens. It is a holiday; gloom must not be allowed to spoil the festival.

Jacob eats. We pretend not to see that he is famished. Father begins a song. "Sing, Johannes!" calls Grandmother.

"Yes, yes, you have the best voice," they all say. I know that the flute is my real voice, but, of course, we cannot play instruments on festivals or Sabbath. So I sing with the others, until they stop and let me carry it alone: "Sing praises to our God, for His kindness endureth forever!"

I am elated. Jacob has come. Oh, the festive farewell when Jacob went away to study. Oh, the grief that swept through the community when Jacob's parents died of typhoid within three days of each other. Reb Meier sent a letter to Jacob, by way of a traveling monk. That was a year ago, and now is the first time Jacob has returned to Strasbourg.

"Are you staying, Jacob?" I ask.

Jacob draws himself up and he sighs. "What can I do here? There is already a Jewish doctor in Strasbourg. I thought I would look around, maybe try in Colmar or Freiburg, maybe even Frankfurt."

"Our physician is old," says Mother. "Perhaps he needs an assistant."

Father looks stern. "You know the quota," he says in a low tone.

"Well, perhaps we could petition the bishop or the council." Mother's hands wave helplessly. "Perhaps the baron would intercede. I've heard there is sickness in his household."

"Don't raise the boy's hopes, Miriam."

"In the old days," says Grandmother, "when the king got sick, remember the story? How they sent for the Jewish doctor all the way from Spain?"

"That was the old days," Grandfather says heavily. He sits back, the posture of remembering. "I don't wish for a return to the old days." Grandfather looks around the table. "The famine. People eating cats and dogs."

"Not the Jews," quips David. "Those animals are not kosher."

We all laugh.

"The Jews ate roots," says Grandfather reproachfully.

"Enough, Papa," says Grandmother. The lines on her face make her appear to be smiling even when she is not. "These children have heard enough about our hardships and the past. Let them be happy!"

"It is good for them to know," Grandfather insists. "Let them appreciate what they have here. Protection from Bishop Berthold himself, may he stay on the path of justice!"

"How is the dear bishop?" asks Jacob, rolling his eyes.

"Well, as ever," replies David. "They say he has relaid his floors in marble all the way from Italy."

I add, "The bishop's fingers are laced with rings."

Father's lips are taut. The bishop collects the Jew tax. Father worries, always, that he will raise it once again. But Grandfather remains undeterred in his sudden rush of gratitude, and he raises his goblet, declaring loudly, "To our friend Jacob! To a good year, a year of learning and of good works. And may we prosper at the fair!"

I am amazed. I have heard talk of the fair at Troyes, but no decisions yet. Father would go to change and lend money. Is it possible that he would take me with him? I feel that rush of excitement, trying to conceal it as I ask, "We are going to the fair, then?"

"Not 'we,'" replies Father swiftly. "Grandfather and I, and perhaps David, if he wishes."

I feel smitten and shamed. My face burns.

"It might be good business to take the boy," puts in Uncle David. "If he is to learn . . ."

Father only frowns and drums his fingers on the table. He is still angry over Zorn's accusation, I know. He holds it in, but I can see his thoughts against me. It fills me with wrath.

"They are holding the summer fair?" asks Jacob.

"Why not?" asks Grandfather.

"Well, there was talk in Paris about fairs being unhealthy, and maybe canceled altogether. Because of the pestilence in the south of France."

Rochele says, "In the square today we heard a friar talking about hell and sin and pestilence."

"What were you doing in the square?" Mother wants to know.

"Why were the children out today?" Father inquires.

"They went for water."

"What were they doing by the cathedral? Why did you not send Johannes for water?"

"He went to fetch the children. How could I know—?"

"You mean to tell me that you let Rochele—"

"*Sha, sha.*" Grandmother tries to stop the strife; but it is too late.

"From now on," shouts Father, "the children do not go out unless—"

Rochele, frightened, interrupts. "Herr Betscholt and Baron Zorn had it in for Johannes. They knocked off his hat, and they beat him."

All eyes now turn on me. I am furious at Rochele. I want to slap her. "Be still!"

"What did you do, Son?" asks Father. He half rises from his chair. "Were you insolent? Were you proud? Is that why Zorn came here to cheat us?"

The words seem to explode from my mouth. "I followed your rule and was kicked like a dog. Isn't that what you want for me? To grovel in the dust?"

The ugly words, once spoken, cannot be recanted. My heart beats wildly. If it was not a festival, if Jacob was not here, Father would bring down his strap. I don't care! Let the strap fall a hundred times! Father gives me a look, then he points to the door.

I get up and leave. It is unforgivable to display such anger, especially at the festival table, especially in front of a guest. Even Uncle David's face is stormy. God will punish me, I am certain of it. Outside I feel the great chill of the night. I see the brittle stars so far away, like a thousand accusing eyes.

I sit on the low wall, listening to voices from all the houses with their celebrants and songs. Candles flicker. Shadows move along walls. Everyone is happy, except me. Something is bad inside me. Maybe old Saul has a tonic against these dark moods. Maybe I am bewitched, with those terrible dreams of late. I think of the friar's words: *pus, boils, pestilence.* I shiver with dread.

"Come inside, Johannes." Mother is standing in the doorway. Her white kerchief and collar gleam in the moonlight. "You'll catch your death out here. Come."

"Forgive me, Mother." I sigh heavily. "I don't know what gets into me."

"I know," Mother says. "It is the weather—cold and hot, moist and dry. It gets into the soul of a young person. Come now, we have to finish the service. Father has hidden the *matzo.* You can help look for it. The prize is an orange."

Benjamin wins the orange, of course. Rochele's eyes are upon Benjamin as he peels and sections the fruit and holds it in his mouth to capture the flavor. Smiling, Benjamin then sections the rest and passes it along the table. Now I cannot resist the golden fruit and the goodness of my wild little brother. I find myself laughing along with the others, taking the last cup of wine—ah, it is good! And now comes the talk.

"The friar spoke of a pestilence. He said a ship sailed into Messina

Harbor with the entire crew dead or dying, spitting blood and pus. He said it is the result of sin."

"Many students have left Paris. They fear the pestilence may spread."

"How can that be? If, as you say, it is so far away, in Italy and southern France—"

"These things have been known to spread. I remember, in the old days, how the famine brought earthquakes; the quakes caused terrible humors to be let loose in the atmosphere, causing diseases."

"In Paris, some say it is the conjunction of planets. Saturn, Mars, and Jupiter are now in the house of Aquarius. Saturn and Jupiter mean death and disaster. Mars and Jupiter spread pestilence in the air."

"Well, what is being done to protect people?"

"Some lepers have been rounded up, I think, and punished."

"Lepers, again!"

"They are said to have spread pollution. Some were arrested and expelled."

Father and Mother look at each other. "It is late."

Mother says, "The candles are nearly done. Jacob, you will sleep here? You can share Johannes's pallet."

"I am grateful to you. Tomorrow I'll be on my way."

"No work tomorrow," I whisper. "It is a festival day. We can spend it together."

"I'd like nothing better," says Jacob. "Tell me, how is it with the butcher's family?"

"They are well." My mind is suddenly divided, one part swimming with happiness at spending a day with Jacob, the other seething with jealousy. I know that Jacob will ask one more question.

"How is the young daughter, Margarite, the redhead? Is she married yet?"

"No," I say as I feel my heart racing. "Not yet."

CHAPTER SEVEN

I want to see everything and everyone!" Jacob runs outside, heedless of the still frosty air. "But first, to the bath." He puts his arm around my shoulder.

"You are not married yet," I say.

Jacob laughs. "Neither are you!"

"I am only sixteen. You are nineteen. Isn't it time?"

"Indeed! First I have to be able to support a wife. You," he says, standing away to look at me, "you have an occupation, a business with your father."

"Some business!" I tell Jacob of Zorn's visit and his treachery. "The worst is, we will still have to pay a tax to the bishop on all the interest Zorn was supposed to pay."

"Even though he never paid it? That's absurd!"

"That's how it is," I say. "They will inspect the books and say it was paid. They tax us for everything. Grandfather says times are better now, the king protects us, but still . . ." I feel a sudden, intense desire. "I wish I could go to Paris, as you did."

"Paris is very crowded and very filthy," says Jacob.

"I don't care!"

"At least you have work to do."

"Dirty work," I mutter. "The looks they give us—as if we were filth."

"They need you," says Jacob. "The world revolves on business. I wish I knew about it, changing money, giving credit and such. And all those different currencies. How can anyone keep it straight?"

Maybe I know something after all! I tell Jacob, "It starts with silver and gold. We use coins because nobody can carry blocks of silver around. Take the livre—it is made of silver; one pound of it will make 240 silver pennies. Right?"

Jacob shrugs and grins. "If you say so."

"There are twelve pennies to the sou, twenty sou to the livre."

"What about all those others? The ducat, the florin, the franc . . ."

"Well, they are equal to the livre, more or less. This is what we have to know, and it changes week by week, month by month. We just have to learn it."

"How do you learn the changes?"

"It depends what you can buy for the coin—well, it is complicated."

Jacob shakes his head. "These matters make my head ache."

I laugh. "We'll go to Saul, the gardener, and get you a potion."

We walk together, while I wonder whether to tell Jacob. Will he think me foolish or mad? I shrug off the doubts and tell him about my dream, the strange masks. "People in it all had the same faces," I explain. "None were old or ugly. They were . . . perfect. And yet, it was terrifying. What do you make of that, Jacob?"

"I'm a doctor," says Jacob, "not a sorcerer. But it sounds as if you are looking for a perfect world."

"Not so. I do not control my dreams. It frightened me, Jacob, not to see real faces. What could it mean? Is God hiding His face from us?"

"Perhaps it is a prophecy," Jacob says, "and soon *Moshiach* will come, and all men will be perfected, as it says in the Torah."

We walk on toward the bathhouse. I am not accustomed to such serious talk, especially not so early in the morning. I laugh slightly now as I dodge the slops a woman is emptying from an upstairs window.

Jacob continues, "If everyone had the same face, how would you know the people you love? And not to grow old—would people remain young forever? Does that mean they never die, never get to the Garden of Eden?"

"It was only a foolish dream," I say, yet it continues to haunt me.

At the bathhouse we strip and immerse ourselves quickly in the cold water, which flows in from the river. I feel my scalp tingling;

my hands and feet are numb. We shout, then leap out, shivering, slapping ourselves dry, sharing a towel.

Suddenly I want to sing, and I do! *"Ah! De-um-bum-bum,"* and I yodel very nicely, high and low, while Jacob stands there laughing and clapping.

Raucous voices ring out loud and crude. I know that voice. It is Konrad, the butcher's son, with his pals. "Want to know something?" Konrad yells. "They have to bathe all the time because they bleed."

Another one shouts, "Look at them! Now you can see the shape of those devils. Come on, boys! Grab their clothes. Look! Look at that one leaping!"

Five of them pounce into the bathhouse. They swoop upon our clothes, snatch them, tearing the seams. "What do you want?" says Jacob. He is calm. His hands hang at his sides; he is not ashamed of his nakedness.

"We want to see you," says the largest of the boys. "No wonder you are so weak. They have cut a piece of your manhood away. I hear it bleeds every Friday night. Is it true?"

Jacob turns to leave, but I am furious and I shout, "We are not weak!"

"Oh? Prove it," yells Konrad. "How far can you piss with that wounded limb?"

"Farther than you." I want to eat my words; but I am choked with hatred for this Konrad the Snake, whose hair is straight and pale as winter straw.

"Let's see. We'll use the wall. I'll go first."

They line up, cursing.

Konrad Betscholt, the butcher's son, goes first. And it is an impressive stream.

"Now you." He points to me. The others gather around.

I strain. I hold my breath, unprepared for such a contest and doomed to disappointment.

"Two against two," declares Jacob, striding up to the boys. "You," he says to the largest, the leader. "Winner takes all."

"Takes what?" shouts the leader, ready to kick and punch.

"Takes the prize. The honor."

"Loser gets his face washed in the mud," declares Konrad, laughing.

"Agreed," says Jacob. "You want to go first?" he asks the leader.

"Yes," says the leader. "First."

His followers cheer. They measure the distance and are gratified.

"Well, I will stand back here," says Jacob, "and after beginning, I will take a step back, then another step back, and I will still hit the wall!"

"You and the devil!" the five shout derisively, but we all watch in fascination as Jacob makes good his boast. *Thank you, God!* I murmur a silent prayer, even as I wonder whether it is appropriate to thank God for such a victory. I cannot resist a shout of joy. "We won! Now you see!"

It is a mistake. In a moment they catch my arms, pin them behind me, and drag me to the pit, pressing my face down into the cold, odorous mud. Beside me, Jacob is sputtering, too, and then there is only the sound of our spitting and coughing. The five toughs are gone.

I get up and look at Jacob. Laughter bursts from me like a stream, a fountain. We howl and slap at each other, laughing so hard we cannot stand. "We showed them, didn't we!" I exclaim. Glorious victory! I feel like a giant.

"We did. Yes, we did. The pity is we can't tell anyone."

"We don't have to tell. We know. We two."

We rinse ourselves again in the icy water, then dress and run back toward home for *matzo* with eggs and honey.

Jacob has gone to see Rabbi Meier, to hear about the burial for his parents. Together they will walk to the cemetery to visit the graves. Jacob needs to be alone with the rabbi, so there is time for me to be free, to go walking. I bring Rochele along, knowing where my steps will guide me.

We knock at Margarite's door. We hear laughter from inside. Both girls open it, laughing still. "Good afternoon! *Gut yom tov!*" Margarite and Rosa call out.

Margarite's mother is there, offering lemon water and small fried *matzo* cakes.

"It's so dark and hot inside!" Margarite objects. Her look is downcast, but her brown eyes are merry. "Let us fix a basket and we'll take it outside. Rosa and Rochele can come, too."

Of course the little girls want to go. They are already dancing about with delight.

Swiftly the basket is packed—some apples and pecans, the *matzo* cakes, lemon water in a jug stopped with a sturdy rag. "Don't go far!" calls their mother.

"We won't," promises Margarite.

I long to take Margarite's hand, but, of course, I cannot. I match my steps to hers, and my arm grazes her arm as we stroll slowly past the houses and on into the fields, with Rosa and Rochele skipping ahead.

"Was your Seder pleasant?" Margarite inquires.

"Indeed," I say. "Jacob came back."

"I heard."

"He looks very well. He wants to go to Frankfurt or to Basel to be a doctor."

"Frankfurt! So far."

"Would you care, Margarite?" I have not meant to sound so passionate, but my heart is beating wildly, my thoughts are all in confusion. I walk faster. Margarite follows.

"He is your friend," she says. "I only care for your sake." Now she turns, so that we are looking into each other's eyes. I feel that mad pulsing in my entire body. I cannot speak. We walk on.

Beyond the bridge and the high stone towers, the grasses are coming up green and tender. Lambs and cattle graze peacefully, guarded by shepherd boys, who are always secretive and sullen. Margarite stops under a pepper tree and spreads out a cloth of white linen fringed with red-and-white threads.

"Pretty cloth," I compliment, and sit down beside her. The little girls are playing tag around a huge oak.

"I made it," says Margarite. "I was going to embroider it, but . . ." She shrugs. "I am not good for sitting still too long."

"You want to run? Like the children?"

Margarite laughs and pushes back her hair. It is so thick, it must feel like fleece. I keep my hands clasped together.

"No," she says. "I want to plant. I have already made a garden of herbs. Old Saul, the gardener, is teaching me."

"You are a healer," I say, gazing at her. The sun is touching her cheek.

Margarite nods slowly. "I healed my poor mother of leg cramps last week. It is wondrous to see the work that the herbs can do. I believe," she says, her chin lifted slightly, "that there is a remedy for every sickness. We have only to discover it."

"I hope you are right," I murmur, inhaling deeply the fragrances in this meadow. How I would love to lie here in the grass!

"It must be so," says Margarite seriously. "God made the world and everything in it. Surely He also prepared medicines for our well-being, just as He provided food."

"Sometimes food is scarce," I remark.

"Well, yes." Margarite sighs. She begins to unpack the cakes, the apples, and the lemon water. She gives some to the little girls and to me. Margarite has never given me food before. I take it from her hand, murmuring a blessing to myself.

"You made these?" The sweet *matzo* cakes are delicious, filled with raisins and nuts.

"My mother made them. I am not good for—"

"I know." I am grinning. "You are not a cook but a healer."

"You laugh at me."

"No. I—" What can I say? I reach into my pocket. What was I thinking of, or did Satan put the flute there to tempt me? He knows it is forbidden to play instruments on Sabbath or holy days. But now, lovesick, I bring the flute to my lips and begin to play. It is a melody from childhood, only twelve basic notes, but I improvise and elaborate. The notes dance and climb. The little girls come running over, clasping hands, whirling together. Amid the grass are tiny white narcissus and flat-faced dandelions, waving in the breeze as if they, too, are dancing.

Margarite sits, her face aglow, her hands in her lap. And suddenly she leaps up and clasps the hands of the two little girls, spinning with them round and round.

The sun moves in the sky. It is of no account. Nothing needs be done on this day, holy day, day of rest and thanksgiving. But cows must be milked all the same! Into the field, each carrying a bucket, come a woman and her son, both of sturdy peasant stock. The woman sways from side to side as she walks.

"Good day!" she calls, smiling and nodding to us.

"Good day, Greta! Good day, Gunther."

Greta the Winker, as she is called from her habit of blinking one eye, milks cows for a living. If an owner is ill or traveling, he calls Greta the Winker and her son, Gunther. Their pay is a small portion of milk, which Greta the Winker uses for making cheese. On Sabbath and holy days, Greta and her son milk the cows belonging to Jews, including the one Holstein owned by Margarite's father. It is a kindness repaid by kindness; the cow's udders are painfully full and must be relieved. The Sabbath milkers may keep the milk for themselves.

"So, I wish you all a happy holiday," says Greta, squinting against the sun.

Gunther stops and smiles. "Hullo, Johannes," he says. "We heard your flute. It is very beautiful, what you can do."

Greta the Winker winks. "You are a sorcerer, to make people dance, even an old woman like me. I almost took this boy by the arm and did a turn or two!"

"Thank you, thank you," I say, nodding, tucking my flute away. Margarite and I watch them go down the road.

"A nice woman," says Margarite. "She is gentle with the cow."

"If only they were all that way," I say, wishing I hadn't said it.

"I can't bear the slaughtering," Margarite suddenly bursts out. "Our cow—I have named her Channie. Father promised me he will never slaughter her but"—she sighs—"we have to eat."

"It is a milch cow, isn't it?" I say to soothe her. "He won't slaughter a milch cow."

"I have seen his face," Margarite says, "when he makes the cut. He winces. His face is all furrowed. How can he go on doing it year after year?" She turns to me, eager. "I have a plan," she says, "to grow so many vegetables that we won't have to eat meat."

"What about Sabbath and holidays?" I ask. "What about Passover? We are supposed to eat a lamb." Now I can see that she does not want logic; she is upset, turning away from me, her hands over her face.

"Oh, Margarite. I'm sorry."

She is weeping.

"What is it?" I can't bear to see her tears. "Have I said something terrible? If so, please forgive me!"

Margarite shakes her head. "I am ashamed, Johannes, for sometimes when I see the animal blood on my father's hands, I do not want to touch him or even look at him."

I am struck by sudden understanding. "I know!" I exclaim. "Look at me. I have to be a moneylender, like my father. It sickens me. If I could do anything, go anyplace . . ."

"What would you do?" Margarite asks.

"I would make music. I would travel beyond the river and play my flute. But the world is—it is . . ." I cannot find words for my discontent.

"I do not like it," Margarite says stubbornly. "Come, girls," she calls sharply.

"I will tell you something," I say as we begin to walk. "Once, when I was out very early by the east bridge, I saw something. I have never told anyone about it, not even my father."

Margarite slows her steps. "What did you see?"

"A man standing on the bridge with a bundle in his arms. I was half concealed under the bridge in the shadows. The man leaned way over and threw something into the river. He saw me, and there was a terrible expression on his face, as if he meant to kill me. I saw that the blanket was still in his hands, and the bundle—the baby— was sinking very slowly down."

Margarite stares at me, her brown eyes filling with tears. She whispers, "Why didn't you tell your father?"

"Because I know what he would have said; that this is what some people do when a child is sick or they cannot afford to feed it. It is the way of the world, and we cannot change it."

We walk silently for a time, each taking our little sister by the hand. The little girls have become sober, too. I give Rochele's hand a squeeze.

"Maybe we can change it," Margarite says.

It begins at dusk, that time when sounds and shadows play tricks on people. The first sound is a swift rustling and scraping, as if things are being gathered. Jacob and I, playing chess, do not bother to hear; we are engrossed. Jacob is winning, then I am ahead. We are well matched.

Something hits the wall with a thud. Jacob leaps up. "What was that?"

Mother pulls Rochele away from the window. Grandmother stares fixedly, immobile in her chair. "The rabble," she mutters. "It's started."

"Where is your father?" asks Mother.

"He and Grandfather went out to visit Zemel, the baker," I say.

"Oh, my God!"

"I'll run and tell them," says Jacob.

He is already out the door, and I follow, while Mother shouts, "Be careful!"

Zemel's house is two streets up. We must hurry along the back alley to get back home before the melee. Our feet hardly seem to touch the ground. I feel an immense surge of strength.

We pound on Zemel's door, gasping. "Come home! It's started."

Father and Grandfather hastily leave; they both run, the old man hobbling. I take Grandfather's arm, pulling him along. I would carry him if I could!

Now things are flying in the air. Sticks and stones. A bag of excrement. A small flaming torch is hurled against a wall. As it lands, Father and I stamp it out. Crude, cursing voices collide with the crashing of stones and bricks and pieces of iron. Amid the shattering noise, some words ring out clearly, "Killed our Lord! Killed our Lord! Jews in league with the devil."

A cart is smashed into pieces. A barrel goes rolling crazily down the street, crashes into a post. Rocks hit houses, breaking off bits of plaster. Urns split apart, and flower pots and a peddler's wagon. The wares burst out onto the street, and the marauders shout their victory. A woman scurries into a doorway, dragging two children with her. A dog barks hysterically. A large stone smacks against its head. The animal staggers back, stunned, then drops.

Several adults watching seem slightly amused, indulgent: Boys will be boys; it is tradition, this Holy Week ruckus. Some of the boys wear clerical garb. They are students at the monastery. They have learned that Jews still refuse to accept Christ as Lord, that they threaten all Christendom with their heresies. Haven't they committed unspeakable crimes? Yes, yes; they murder Christian children and drain out their blood. They take the Host wafers and torture them. It comes from reliable sources—a priest in Alsace swears he saw a Jew beating a wafer until it bled.

Father and I hold Grandfather tightly, shielding him; but Jacob, running ahead, is their chosen target. "Look! Get him. That's the one!"

Jacob falls. Blood seeps from his nose, and from his ear. Jacob cannot move. His eyes stare out blankly.

Somehow we gather him up and get him into the house, with the madness increasing, now that it is night. Flames are leaping, for many torches blaze. A haystack is set on fire. "Serves him right! Filthy foreigner! Come on, boys, to the cemetery. Let's dig up their ghosts!"

In the house, Jacob retches. He cannot stand. The women surround him, wipe him with damp cloths, and Grandmother weeps and lifts her hands, first in anguish, then in prayer.

How has this disaster come upon us?

I feel that terrible heaviness in my chest, reaching to my very soul. I am responsible. It was I who proposed the contest in the first place. But worse yet, I knowingly violated the holy day with my flute—I was arrogant; I was willful.

And it is my best friend, Jacob, who has to pay.

CHAPTER
EIGHT

I am consumed with joy. I am going to the fair! Murmurs in the night, like transparent images, floated into my dreams—"A good lad . . . let him go . . . needs to learn . . ." And one morning Father told me in few words, "You are coming with us to the Hot Fair to work and to learn."

I force myself to remain calm and silent, but inside I am bursting with excitement. None of my friends has journeyed beyond the river, except for Jacob. Most people, like Greta and Gunther, have never ventured beyond the village green. Do they envy me? Or do they think I am strange because I long to know what lies beyond the forest, what manner of people, what sights?

I wish Jacob could come with us to the fair, but he has not recovered from that terrible night. An ugly red clot has formed on his skull, and he grows dizzy and faint.

The four of us make a small procession—I, with Father and Grandfather and Uncle David. Before we can leave Strasbourg, we must settle our taxes. I feel the pride of business as we stride through the narrow streets, out onto the main *gasse*, or thoroughfare, over the bridge (the same bridge where I had watched the killing of an infant), then on to the quay and the grand customhouse.

Outside, with a large meat-stuffed roll in one hand and a thick walking staff in the other, stands Count Engelbracht. His staff is tipped with gold. Count Engelbracht's leather purse hangs from his belt. Like his belly, it bulges.

I have never seen Count Engelbracht when he was not either eating or conferring with a clergyman. Today he is doing both, and it is with the bishop himself!

Engelbracht is a master of a large estate. Nobody knows for certain how many peasants eat their daily rations by his favor. Now his hand is on Bishop Berthold's arm. The two men are talking earnestly, gesturing with their hands. Their brows are furrowed from important business.

We pass, keeping our eyes down.

"Good day!" the bishop calls, tilting his head challengingly. He lifts his arm in a noble gesture, showing his fur-lined sleeve.

"Good day," Father answers.

Count Engelbracht picks up the inquiry. "You have business here in council chambers?"

"We come to pay our taxes, Your Honor," says Father.

"Very well." The count stands aside, seems about to question us further, but changes his mind. "Very well," he repeats. "Go in."

Inside in the vast, chilly room, Peter Swarber, the distinguished, dark-haired assessor, sits behind a massive table. There has always been a Swarber on the town council. I feel awestruck in the presence of such an important man. He is not arrogant, like some others. Peter Swarber's arms rest on the table, piled with books and charts. Behind him, set into dark paneling, is an enormous fireplace, now cold and empty. A thin-faced assistant hovers deferentially beside Peter Swarber, eyes darting and eager.

The assistant announces us. "Menachem the Jew, moneylender, his father and son. And David the Jew, money changer."

I stand stock-still behind my father. I am carrying the ledger, glad for the shield of my father's back. This room, with its dark woods and cold, silent hearth, makes me shiver, even though it is summer now and outside the sun is blazing.

Peter Swarber looks up. His mouth is pleasant, his gaze distant. "What service?" he asks.

"We have come to pay our taxes before leaving town. We are bound for the fair at Troyes."

The councilman-assessor, Peter Swarber, takes out his logbook. "You are going for purposes of trade as well as money changing?"

Peter Swarber asks formally, although he obviously knows.

"Yes," says Father. "Several neighbors have asked us to take goods for them to the fair."

Peter Swarber's eyebrows lift. "Gentile neighbors?" he asks.

"Some gentiles, yes," says Father. "Frau Greta, Herr Closener, and also some fellow Jews."

"You are, of course, prepared to pay the additional tax on this trade," says Swarber, nodding to his assistant, who picks up a quill.

"Of course," Father says.

I try to calculate what it will cost to change our Strasbourg money into other coinage. For the fair, we will need gold florins and groschen, a large quantity of silver denier, the thin coin that can be cut in half, and even into quarters if necessary. The taxes are staggering. No wonder Father says there is little left after all is done.

Peter Swarber watches his assistant count out the coins. Mere money, his look implies, means nothing to him. He subtracts the fee and passes the piles of coins to Father across the table.

Father glances at the coins and quickly counts them. Uncle David scoops them into a large leather bag slung over his shoulder. The muscles in his arms bulge. Uncle David also hides a dagger in his belt, security on the long trek to Troyes beginning tomorrow morning.

Outside again, we pass the bishop, now seated alone on a bench, feeding pigeons. He looks up. Father pauses and murmurs, "Your Excellency."

"Be sure," says Bishop Berthold, still nurturing the pigeons, "that before you leave Strasbourg your head tax is paid."

"I have already given it to Rabbi Meier, Your Excellency," says Father with a slight bow.

"Due to my continued efforts," says the bishop, "you and your commerce have been protected. I have always been a friend to the Jews." He tosses out a handful of crumbs and wipes his hand on his gown. Several gorgeous rings gleam from the folds of the bishop's thick fingers. A large emerald set with diamonds shines like a green eye.

"We are indeed grateful!" exclaims Grandfather. "It is well known, Your Excellency, how you interceded for us and attained an armistice with the Armleather gang. Our people pray for your continued health, Your Excellency."

Bishop Berthold waves his hand, his head inclined. I see his slight, sardonic smile. "Yes, well. We pray also," he says, "for your souls."

My face burns at this barb, but I must keep silent, eyes downcast. Grandfather still smiles. Father nods, and Uncle David stands silently by, clutching the bag with the coins.

But Bishop Berthold is not quite finished. I feel his hand on my shoulder, and my spirit turns to ice. He says, "I see you have a son to follow in your footsteps, Menachem."

"Yes, Your Excellency," says Father. "He is a good son."

"See to it," says the bishop as he turns to walk away, "that he keeps proper accounts."

I feel a raging inside of me. How I despise this bishop! Grandfather says it is wrong to hate. But I have feelings. The bishop made an armistice with the Armleather thugs, who stormed the countryside beating up Jews and wrecking markets. Yes, the thugs agreed to hold their peace for the next ten years. And in exchange for being left alone, the Jews were compelled to pay a tax of one thousand denier yearly to the bishop. Perhaps the bishop encouraged the thugs all along, so he could get the credit for making peace. Why doesn't Grandfather see it? Father has told the bishop that I am a good son. Does he mean it, or is it another lie to placate the bishop?

At home, Mother and Grandmother are packing our things—extra cloaks, a blanket, a water jug, and, of course, food: some salted fish, flat cakes wrapped in an oiled cloth, apples, and nuts.

"We don't need all this food," says Father, shaking his head.

"You never know," says Oma. "What if the friends you know have moved away?"

"We can always buy fruits and vegetables from vendors," says Father, laughing. "Don't worry, we can take care of ourselves."

"Take care of your father," she says with a sniff. "A man his age, going on such a trip! People will think he is crazy."

Grandfather only nods, grinning. "So, I'm crazy. One last time, I go to the fair. Besides, Menachem needs me."

"I certainly do," says Father. "You are the fastest and best money changer in the land. You know the trades, the people, the road—"

"Thank you, my son. But we all know you are only being kind, and I will slow you down."

"We are bringing the donkey," says Father.

"What donkey?"

"Borrowed from Elias, the butcher."

A donkey! We go in style, then, with a donkey to carry supplies, and when Grandfather is tired he can ride. I go to Father. He already knows what I want. "Yes, you will go and fetch the donkey," he says. "Don't tarry. You must be home before dark. Also you must stop at Greta's house for her cheeses, and go to Herr Fritsche Closener, too. He told me he has some documents to bring."

I feel almost dizzy with importance. And Benjamin begins to wail. "I want to go to the fair, Papa! Why should I stay home?"

"We have talked about this," Father said sternly. "You will be needed here. You are nearly grown, the man of the house while we are gone."

"Johannes always goes with you!"

"Johannes is the eldest. Hush, now!" Father says.

"We will bring you a present from the fair," says Uncle David. "What do you want?"

"A horse," says Benjamin. His gaze is still fierce.

"Now, Benjamin . . . ," Mother says.

"I want a horse," says Benjamin, his voice rising. "We need a horse. You know we do, Mama! If we had a horse we could—"

"If we had a palace . . . ," says Grandfather, laughing, and Oma joins in. "If we had a golden bird . . ."

Benjamin is holding in his tears, I can tell. "If we had a horse," Benjamin whispers, "I would tend it. Johannes and I could go and trade for the family. Like Grandfather did in his youth. We would not have to be moneylenders only—if we had a horse!" he cries out from the deep in his soul.

Father bends down near to Benjamin. I do not know whether he will slap Benjamin or kiss him. "We have no money for a horse," he says softly. "You know that."

"Maybe you will do well at the fair," mutters Benjamin.

"If we get rich at the fair," says Father in a tone of finality, "you will get a horse." He turns to Rochele. "What shall we bring you, little one?"

I know what Rochele wants. I have heard her prayers in the night. Real shoes, she desires, of leather, beautiful and soft. Until now she has worn only sandals made at home.

"A ribbon," says Rochele. "And perhaps a sweet. Please."

Father kisses her brow, then motions to me. We stand in the alcove, divided by a curtain, where the money boxes and pledges and ledgers are kept. Father gazes at me sternly. He brings down the strongbox, counts out six silver coins, and places them in my hand.

"Take these to Elias," he says, "and bring back his donkey."

"I thought you said—"

"Hush. Elias is a proud man. He does not want it known that he had to sell his donkey in order to live."

I whisper, "But I've heard it said that butchers and bakers will always have food on the table—and grave diggers, too."

We laugh together, it is a good moment, warm and pleasant. Then Father grows sober again. "Well, he has had trouble, you know, with the other butchers, for selling the cuts we can't eat. Hindquarters, anything bruised, he must sell to gentiles, and, of course, he gives them a good price."

"So I suppose they will make a law that gentiles cannot buy meat from Jews." There is great bitterness in my tone.

"Oh, that has been law for a long time. Most gentiles don't heed it. But still, the butchers are furious at being undersold. So they have other means of keeping their business. You know how it is. You are almost fully a man, my son. You must understand these things."

I sigh and nod. My expression feels new to me, and I think it must be like that of the other men when they are helpless against injustice. I think also of Margarite's words about wanting to change the world. I tell Father, "I'll go now for the donkey."

"Take Benjamin with you."

Benjamin goes gladly on this manly errand. Out on the road he asks, "What happens if Christians don't follow the law and buy from Elias?"

I give my brother a slight shove. "So you always listen?"

"I'm not deaf!"

"Well, I guess they threaten people, maybe beat them. Who knows?"

"I hate those butchers!" Benjamin bursts out. "That Konrad, the butcher's son—remember what he did to Rochele?"

"I cannot forget," I say. "Look, let's not talk about that. Here is Herr Closener's place." I knock. In a moment the door is opened. The large head of a hound thrusts itself out, and Benjamin drops to his knees, enchanted.

"Ho! What a beauty. A beautiful hound—look at those ears! What is his name?"

"Her name is Wechsel," says a deep voice, and Herr Closener stands before us. His face is furrowed from his profession, his skin bronzed; and the lines on his face fall into a smile. He is a scribe and a teacher, known for his library—it is said that he owns more than forty books!

"Come in! Come in!" he says cordially, leading us into the small but substantial house with its floors of dark wood, a sleeping alcove and its high trundle bed, a little table and hearth, over which hang iron utensils and cooking pots. Everything is neatly kept. Most prominent is the scholar's desk, cluttered with notes and drawings, maps, writing instruments, and parchment.

"It is most good of your father," says Closener, rummaging through his desk, "to do this for me. I have been corresponding with a monk in Troyes about . . . well, he will be glad to get these papers. We are compiling a history of the region, and I have contributed— never mind. You boys would rather be on your way instead of listening to a foolish scribbler."

"Not at all, sir!" I exclaim. I see a recorder on the shelf, and a beautiful lute. "Do you play, sir?"

"A little," says the man. He reaches for the recorder. "And you?"

"I attempt to play the flute."

"My brother is too modest," cries Benjamin. "He plays beautifully!"

"You must come sometime," says Closener, "and we will play together. Perhaps you can teach me some new melodies? I always like it, very much, to learn new melodies."

"And I, too." I feel breathless from the wonder of it.

"Then we will see each other after the fair," says Closener with a nod and a broad smile. He hands me the papers, bound together with string. Benjamin is once again on his knees, stroking the hound. The dog wets Benjamin's cheeks with kisses.

"Indeed, you have a way with animals," I tell my brother when we are again outside. "What would you do with a horse?"

"Brush it, ride it, stroke it, feed it. And we would go places together, you and I." Now I hear the burning desire in Benjamin's voice, and I know it is not only the horse that Benjamin desires but time, more time, with his brother. I have felt such feelings myself, when Uncle David had no time for me.

"When we return from the fair," I promise my brother, "when it is autumn and winter, we will do things together. We can walk in the woods and gather berries and nuts and pine boughs."

"Ha," says Benjamin. "That is for girls—or for lovers. You can gather berries with Margarite," he says boldly.

I smile and clap him on the back. "Well, then, we can read and study and tell tales. If you could play the lute—"

"My fingers won't play, you know that," says Benjamin, stretching out his hands. Indeed, Benjamin has the hands of a peasant, doughy and rough, not the slender and supple hands of a musician.

We have come to the home of Elias, the butcher. Out back, in a small enclosed yard filled with weeds and a pile of animal bones, a donkey is tethered to a fence that surely could not hold him if he balked. But the animal stands patiently, and it gazes at us as we approach.

Benjamin immediately strokes the animal's muzzle.

"Be careful!" I call. "Maybe it bites."

"No, no," murmurs Benjamin. "This is a sweet animal, a peaceful animal."

Suddenly there comes from the lean-to a sonorous chanting, "Blessed art Thou, Lord our God, king of the universe." Then, a single grunt and the sound of a swift struggle. Then, silence. Benjamin and I stare at each other. We wait. By and by Elias comes out from the lean-to half hidden behind the house, together with the *shochet*, carrying the carcass of a goat. The *shochet*'s hands are still stained from his task—to make the first and final cut, along with ritual prayers. Both men are smeared with blood, both are sober, almost sorrowful. Carefully the two men hoist the carcass up onto a wooden slab, where the butcher proceeds to slit the animal's belly with a swift, sure motion, removing the sinews and cutting out the organs. Swiftly the hindquarter is severed, to be sold separately to gentiles. The two men examine the entrails for purity, breathing heavily, intent on their task. Slaughtering is holy work; each man watches the other, their hands moving together. It is an ancient dance.

Elias, the butcher, finally looks up. "Good day, Johannes, Benjamin," he says, speaking slowly, as if breath were precious. "I did not know you had arrived. Please, come into the house and visit. My wife will give you a glass of cider."

"By your leave, sir, Father has asked us to return home before dusk," I say. "We have come for the donkey." I let him see the small sack of coins. "We leave at daybreak tomorrow."

"And may you prosper in your business," says Elias. "One moment, please." He steps to the bucket, dips in his hands up to the elbows, scrubbing himself with rough soap until his arms are red. He nods over the sack of coins, thanking me with a smile.

The slaughterer wipes his knife clean, then murmurs his farewell. Benjamin and I bow slightly to this learned man, wise in the ways of the Torah.

Elias turns and calls into the house. "Margarite! Come out here!" No answer.

He turns to us. His face has gone crimson. "She is unwilling," he says, "to look upon the slaughter." He sighs. "You know how girls are. The Almighty must know I needed sons to help with this work.

Who can say what He intends by giving me two daughters? Well, one must not complain."

I only nod.

"Still," says the butcher, "a girl must obey her father. Margarite!" he shouts, louder this time. "Come out here immediately, I tell you!"

Margarite emerges, tying a scarf over her red hair. "I'm sorry, Papa," she says in a hushed voice. "I did not hear you the first time."

"Then how do you know I called twice?" he retorts, but he gazes upon her with pleasure. Ah, she is so beautiful!

"I have been thinking," says Elias, "about Jacob, the young doctor—is he well enough to work?"

"He seems well enough," I reply. "He has been staying with us or with Dovie or Sampson Pine. He has many friends here who do not want him to leave."

"I can give him work," says Elias. "He knows about bones and joints and such things, doesn't he? He can learn to help me cut the meat. I am entitled to one helper but have not found anyone capable. Jacob could sleep in this shed and he could eat at my table."

My heart is racing. Margarite merely looks down at the ground.

"See to our guests," says Elias, going inside the house. Benjamin runs immediately to the donkey and speaks into its ears in some special language.

Margarite looks over her shoulder as she moves toward a stone bench. Her eyes bid me to follow. "See my herb garden," says Margarite, pointing to the small plot neatly laid out in squares and separated by low stone borders.

"You made this?" I am amazed. "The walls, too?"

Margarite laughs. "Of course! I'm not one to sit around—I like to do things."

"I, too." I laugh out loud. "I'm going to the fair at Troyes! Shall I bring you a present?" I feel bold as a knight, ready to conquer anything for my lady.

"You can take some of my herbs," Margarite says, "and sell them for me. Look! I prepared some in small packets—rosemary for growing hair and keeping away evil, sorrel to use for fever, and nettles and dandelion—"

"I will take whatever you give me," I say. The words come so naturally, though I have never spoken such before. "I will treasure it, because it is from you."

Margarite blushes. Then she frowns and says, "You must take care. Jacob says the pestilence has struck southern France. People die quickly and horribly."

"I know, but Troyes is in the north, very far away." She must care for me, that she worries! "There is nothing to worry about, Margarite. I will bring you a cloth of crimson wool," I say rashly. "It will be beautiful and soft."

Margarite smiles and hands me a small lace handkerchief. I press it to my nostrils, inhaling the fragrance that also clings to Margarite's hair and hands. I am humbled at Margarite's goodness. She wishes to heal the whole world with her herbs.

"*Grüss Gott*," we tell each other. "Go with God."

CHAPTER
NINE

The last stop is at Greta's place, a poor hovel surrounded by rocks and a few gnarled trees, the bottomland of the vast Engelbracht estate. The Engelbracht family is powerful in Strasbourg; still, they are debtors, always living beyond their means. "It is what keeps us in business!" Grandfather says, laughing; but Father frowns when their name is mentioned. They never want to repay their loans.

We tie the donkey to a rail in front of Greta's hut, where she is bent over a furrow, weeding corn. It is a thin crop, but she looks up at us with a smile and a wink. "Ah, you have come for my cheeses, bless you. Maybe some coins will land in my hands after all!"

"We'll do our best, Frau Greta," I assure her.

"You are the best salespeople, I declare it," says Greta. She whistles shrilly for her son to bring the wares. Gunther emerges in a moment from the house, a wooden structure that looks ready to cave in. I am sure it is a miracle that the door even closes, so derelict is this building.

Pride shines in Greta's face as she shows us her cheeses wrapped in cloth. She opens one. It is fat and round, the color of pure cream, studded with valuable spices. "These should bring a fine price," says she. "It will have to last me a long while."

"Why is that?" I know by her glance and her posture that Frau Greta is in need of conversation.

"Engelbracht," she says, jerking her head toward the large manor house on the hill. "He says the milk from two of his cows has dried up, all because of me."

Gunther stands beside his mother, his expression fierce. "It is not true," he mutters.

"What isn't?" asks Benjamin.

"They say it is because we milked the cows of the Jews. They say our hands were contaminated and dried up the udders of their cows." Gunther lifts his chin defiantly. "My mother is not a witch."

"No!" I cry. "Certainly not!"

"They are crazy," says Greta, thumbing her nose. "They can eat worms, for all I care." She winks, but I see the deep lines on her brow. How will she live if she cannot milk cows? This small patch of land cannot feed her and Gunther and the husband inside, who can neither work nor even walk.

"We'll sell your cheeses," I tell her.

Greta reaches into her sleeve. She brings out a coin, a half dinar. "If you would be so kind as to bring me some sugar. Whatever the coin will buy, I would be most grateful."

Benjamin and I each carry away a large pail loaded with cheeses. Benjamin sighs. "What will become of her?"

"She must be careful," I say. "If she is indeed a witch, they will burn her."

"But mustn't there be a trial?"

"I suppose so." I feel suddenly much older, too old. "In France they burned many lepers without any trial," I reluctantly tell my brother. He, too, must know the ways of the world.

"Why? Why?" cries Benjamin. He is walking alongside the donkey, his hand on the animal's flank.

"Grandfather told me about it. They said the lepers were spreading the disease, trying to make everyone sick by poisoning the water. Some lepers were tortured to make them confess."

"What did they do to them?"

"I—they did bad things," I say. No need to explain about the rack and iron tongs, about twisted fingernails and broken bones. Everyone learns about evil soon enough.

"Well, what happened then?" asks Benjamin, his voice high pitched and strange.

"They threw the lepers out of France, just like they expelled the Jews later. Some of the lepers, though, didn't want to go; so they caught them and burned them."

"I will never go to France," says Benjamin defiantly. "Even if Father asked me, I would not go to Troyes."

I know that is not true, but why argue? Benjamin likes to have the last word. Let him.

There is no such a day as the beginning of a journey. I wake up singing and hurry to the morning prayers, standing beside Father and Grandfather, swaying as they do. Suddenly I understand things that before seemed strange—how Abraham, the patriarch, rushed out in the morning to take his son Isaac up to the mountain to do God's bidding. It must have been just such a morning as this, filled with freshness and sunshine, with everything ready and excitement in the air.

Mother takes me aside. "Keep your feet dry," she says seriously. "And do not eat from the stalls."

"Of course I would not!" I am shocked by the thought.

"Look after your grandfather, that he does not overdo—you know how the men behave when they are far from home."

I cannot help smiling. "And am I not a man, too?"

Mother lays her hand on my cheek. "You are sensible, and you are my son." She reaches into her sleeve and gives me a very small parchment, exquisitely lettered. "Take this, my son. Use it. Don't forget."

I take a deep breath, overcome by her trust. I glance at this prayer for the wayfarer, that God may keep us safe from bandits and wild beasts and all evil things that come to earth.

"I got this from my father when I came to be your father's bride," she says.

"You were only fourteen?" Of course, I know the story.

She nods, and her gaze is distant. Her sudden smile is beautiful. "Fourteen. When they cut my hair, it was down to my waist."

"Margarite is sixteen," I say.

My mother laughs. " 'Tis time she thought about marriage, then!"

"Maybe she does not want to get married yet. Margarite is not like other girls. She does not only want to sew and bake!"

"Bread you can always buy," says Mother with a broad smile. "Margarite is a clever girl, a gentle girl. She will be good with her children."

"Who said anything about children?" I grumble. I feel suddenly flushed. Now I remember, and I tell her, "I had the oddest dream last night, Mother. It was about children—such strange children! They were all in sets of twins, male and female."

"What could it mean?" she asks. "Tell me more."

"They lived in a kind of children's house, all together, without any parents. And if they quarreled or raised their voices or said anything harsh—"

" 'Harsh'?" she repeats, looking perplexed.

"Then they were punished. If they sang or danced or tried to make things, they received a—a jolt. It hurt. Something burned their feet. They were always barefoot, so that they could be corrected thus. When I woke up, my foot was hurting dreadfully."

"You must have slept twisted, with your foot under yourself. Twins—I must ask Frau Freda what it means, dreaming of twins. Perhaps it is good luck, double luck for your trip. Don't think about it. 'Twas only a dream."

Farewells and kisses—Mother and Oma and Rochele and Benjamin stand by the door as, proudly, we go, the donkey saddled and packed with our things. Uncle David is stamping impatiently, the skin bag slung over his arm, and a water bag, too. Jacob, who has been with us the night, comes to say good-bye. He clasps my arms, saying, "I'm going to help Elias, the butcher. Strange work for a physician, isn't it? Well, one must make a living. Are you taking your flute along?"

"Of course, I will play on the way. Father says there are minstrels and shows, jesters and mimes."

"I wish I were going," murmurs Jacob. He glances over his shoulder, where the men are making their last-moment preparations. "Do you have lodging on the way?"

"Oh, yes. Father and Grandfather know everyone." I know I should not boast, but this is like no other day in my life. "There are several inns run by Jews. But the weather is fine. We can always sleep in a field."

Father rushes out, rubbing his hands together. "Come, come! Why are we standing here? Let's go!"

We are laden with packs of food and extra clothing. David pulls a wooden cart filled with a strange assortment of objects: some armor left as a pledge and never claimed, which Grandfather has skillfully repaired, along with several swords and a coat of mail. A time or two, when Father was out, I crept in and tried on these things and became instantly transformed into a knight! In the small clouded mirror that Mother keeps on the shelf, I saw myself, splendid and strong, no longer Johannes the Jew but Johannes the rescuer. I told Jacob about it once, and he laughed, then said, "Well, it is merry to be someone else for a while, isn't it? Of course, I've never heard of a Jewish boy playing the part of a knight."

Father will sell the armor at the open-air market, along with other items left and never redeemed: small painted chests, a woman's tiara, several fine cooking pots and utensils. I am joyful as I walk. Music seems to lift my feet.

We join a stream of other travelers, their animals packed to the limit, sides bulging with wares. The weavers, cobblers, tilers, chandlers, and coopers all come laden with products: cloth of blue and crimson, leather sandals and shoes, tiles for small ovens, candles of beeswax, barrels for storage. It seems incredible, like a moving city, a train of products and people, all shouting to their animals or to passersby, raising a trail of dust and debris, scattering the renegade pigs and cats and chickens in their path.

All day we trudge in the dust, Grandfather calling to other merchants, "Ho, there! From where do ye hail?" From all the towns roundabout—Colmar and Freiberg and Basel—and even as far away as Frankfurt they come, bringing their wares and their holiday spirits. Grandfather, enlivened by a taste of his former trading days, smacks his lips and chews on long blades of grass as he engages each passerby in talk of other years and other fairs.

Sometimes the roads are so laden that the dust chokes me. Sometimes we are quite alone, and then I see into the forest, where people are often lost or eaten by wolves. I stay carefully on the path. Among the trees—aspen and oak and pine and wild cherry—the air is cool and sweet. One night we camp in a meadow spread with bright wildflowers. In the morning we are beset by bees—all of us stung— and I wonder: Must every pleasure be paid for by pain?

For four days we have enough to eat, with the provisions from home. Then hunger begins to gnaw at my belly, as a rat gnaws on rope. Food peddlers dot the countryside with their carts, but we dare not eat from them. They offer salted pork and biscuits made with lard and other things that are forbidden to Jews. At the sight of standing wheat and corn and cabbages, I almost become a thief. I see a wormy apple on the ground, swipe it up, and eat it in haste, barely remembering to say the blessing.

"Do not eat the worms," says Uncle David, laughing.

"Am I the only one starving?"

"You are a growing lad," says David.

At night we camp in a field filled with stones. "Where is the inn that Grandfather told us about?" I ask. My bones ache for a bed.

"Soon," says Father. "You must learn patience, my son."

I wish we could stay at a regular inn, but I dare not say so. No proper Jew would stay at a gentile inn. We must rise and bathe in the morning, stand for the daily prayers, recite blessings after eating—and then there is the food itself. Even an egg can be tainted, if it is fried with pig fat.

At last we reach the inn run by Grandfather's friend, but the place is so full that everyone must take turns at the table and at the water pail. What an assemblage of people! There are cloth dyers whose hands are forever stained red, wine makers, glassblowers, even a casket maker. They come from all parts of Germany and Switzerland and southern France.

The innkeeper runs to and fro, shaking out blankets, commanding more straw to be brought for bedding, ordering his daughter to fetch more ale, more bread, more pudding. The girl resembles her father.

Both have dark pouches beneath their eyes. But the girl's lips are full and bloodred.

After a supper of mutton stew and bread, washed down with beer, the talk turns, as always, to commerce. The moneylenders complain. Many would prefer to work in the trades but are banned from practicing them. The Church has strengthened its rule that lending money for interest is sinful; and if Christians are not allowed to lend, who else is left but the Jews? They understand matters of money and commerce, due to their wanderings. It is unlawful for them, too, to bleed the poor. However, it is a kindness to lend money to a brother in need. And what about great ventures? Finding trade routes to distant lands? Someone must finance the ships, the mule trains, the food and lodging for the adventures. Without money, without lending and borrowing, the world shrinks to the size of a walnut shell. Grunting, stretching, scratching against the mites that infest the inn, the men agree. Moneylending is necessary. It could even be noble.

As the candles flicker, talk turns to the strange pestilence that stalks like a beast and creeps like mold. Travelers tell horror stories. Rome is shut down. In the countryside, animals run loose and fields lie desolate with nobody to sow or reap. The pestilence has moved to Lyons. Even in Avignon, where the pope has his residence, the pestilence is raging. The pope has barricaded himself in his palace, causing two huge fires to be kept burning day and night. Priests in that city refuse to attend the dying. People must face death without confession. Nor are there burial spaces or coffins enough. Bodies are being dumped into the river.

A Portuguese man, heavy of beard and brows, lifts his finger for attention. He is a traveling notary, one who attests all written transactions at the fair. "Pope Clement," he says, "has issued a bull in this regard, urging calmness." All eyes focus upon this man. He continues. "There have been demonstrations," he says with an ominous lift to his brows. "Fanatics march about the land urging repentance. It often leads to violence."

A listener calls out, jeering, "Let them repent, after all the harm they've done!"

The Portuguese gives him a stern look. "They then gather in public squares and begin to beat themselves into a frenzy."

"Flagellants," murmurs David beside me.

The man continues, his voice rasping. "The pope has condemned them for preying on the Jews. He has also ruled against forcible conversion or killing or taking property of Jews without trial."

"Ah, you see!" cries Grandfather. "Times have changed. Even the pope demands justice for the Jews."

"Unfortunately," says the notary, "the rabble don't listen. They do what they wish, especially if it brings them profit."

We sit in near darkness as the candles burn down into pools of soft wax. Nobody dares to speak further. To talk of the devil is to conjure him up. Suddenly I wish we had never come.

Beds are scarce. Several young boys must sleep outside with the horses and donkeys. Father, Grandfather, and David share a bed. I am given a pallet to share with two strangers. I pull myself together into a ball, afraid to let my limbs touch the others. I have heard of unpleasant occurrences in places like this. In the morning I am stiff and aching. My body is covered with welts from the vicious bites of fleas.

We rise early, offer prayers, take a hasty breakfast of bread dipped in milk, and depart. The innkeeper's daughter brushes her arm against my shoulder. It is the end of inns for us. From now on we will camp out in the fields, and I am glad of it.

All is well. Grandfather is holding up to the journey. He walks for a time, then sits in the cart, with David and me both pulling it. Fortunately, the old man is not too heavy. My legs feel stronger. My stomach is flat and lean. I am hungry most of the time.

One early morning Father sends David and me to buy food from a farmhouse along the way. The woman looks up at us suspiciously. "Usually I do not sell to Jews," she says, biting down on the coins. "My husband makes the business. He is out in the field with my three sons."

David nods and smiles amiably. "Well, thank you, Good Mother. And may you prosper." He picks up the eggs and the sack of grain we have purchased.

I am fuming. "Why did she say that about her husband and sons? I saw nobody about."

"Poor, frightened soul," says David, "thinking we will attack her, warning that she has protection."

"The cabbage looks moldy," I complain, still in a bad humor.

"Sha," says Uncle David. "Be glad we have it! A few nights from now," he adds, "we will be in Troyes—or at least outside the gates—and then! Merriment, let me tell you, music and plays and songs—you will see."

That night we make music. All along the roadside people come and go, quite as if it were daylight. Some stop to listen, to clap their hands, to sing and dance. I have never known such a night, with music all around and the friendliness of folk who, under the cover of darkness, have no fear and no knowledge of persons with dark, pointed hats that signify Jew. Indeed, I have cast off my hat and nobody chides me. I feel the warm breeze in my hair as we sing and play—oh, there is no better life than that of a troubadour!

Later, when we bed down side by side, I whisper with David about the day and its pleasures. In the town where we stopped at noon, David and I went to the well to drink. Several women waited there, all in strange finery, with bodices low and hair done high with ribbons and flowers.

One with a pretty smile and flushed mien came toward us. Her eyelashes fluttered as she gazed sidelong at David. I felt a strange lurching in my body. The woman's bodice was cut out, and I could see the fullness of her white breasts.

"Perhaps in this world of strife," said the woman, smiling prettily, "you are bound for a few moments of pleasure?"

"Ah, my lady," said David, drawing back, "you are too kind to a poor traveler."

She went on. "I have been with Jews before and found them to be most kind. Or do you find me ugly and undesirable?"

David ducked his head in humility. "You do me too great an honor, a beauty such as you. But I must confess, I have a wife at home and four little ones; and in remembering them, I cannot do as my fondest desire would dictate."

"But the young man with you . . ." The woman persisted.

"Ah, he is betrothed," replied David, grasping my shoulder, leading me away.

Now I ask him, "Why did you tell such lies to that bad woman?" David laughs in the darkness and murmurs, "She was not bad, Johannes, only hungry. Many young maids—and even those not so young—seek to make extra money when travelers come to the fair."

"But you told her you are married and with many children." I want to bite back the words, but I cannot. Poor Uncle. He still grieves for Tamara, and for the child that was stillborn, so that he lost them both in a single day.

David sighs. "To spare her feelings, Johannes. And, in truth, while I might find a swift pleasure in it, I do not want to spoil the memory of Tamara. Now, go to sleep."

But I cannot sleep. A strange disturbance has unbalanced me. "David," I say.

"Yes, Johannes?"

"Is it time that I think of being married?"

"If you ask, Johannes, then it is time."

"How will I support a wife? A family needs so many things." I recall my promise to Margarite: cloth of red wool. How shall I manage it?

"You will work, as we all do," says David. "I know it is not in your heart to be a moneylender."

"If only I could live some other way!" I say. "If I could make music for people . . ."

"Many men," says David, "even some of our wisest sages, had to do work they found unpleasant. The great Hillel was a woodcutter by day. Reb Akiba was a shepherd. They would have loved to spend all their time learning and teaching Torah. We do what we must, Johannes, in order to live and to keep our families from going hungry."

"You are right," I say heavily. "I would do any work for the sake of my family." My face burns, for I am only thinking of Margarite.

"Still, you can make music. When we get to Troyes," says David, "we will stand outside the tents where the gentiles make their plays, and we will hear their music and perhaps learn a fine new tune or two. If there is a wedding, they might ask us to play with them."

"But aren't all their songs about Jesu?"

David chuckles in the darkness. "No, not all." He pauses. "It was good tonight," he says, "all together, making music."

"Yes, it was very good." I make a decision: I will learn everything about money changing. I will acquire a reputation for honesty and wisdom and quick transaction. When I become rich, like Jeckelin and Vivelin Rote, I will rent a fine house for Margarite—one with a garden for her herbs—and every night I will play my flute, and people will come to join me in music, and Margarite will dance.

CHAPTER
TEN

F rom far off, I see the great walls of the city, the color of sand, rising some twenty feet high. Even from this distance, the very air is dense with the crush of activity, masses of people atop the walls, with carts and animals. I can already smell the city, its sewage-laden streets, the odors of slaughtering and tanning and roasting and, simply, living.

On the road the frenzy and the noise increase; everyone is in a hurry to arrive first, to set up a booth or rent a stall. For a few lucky ones, I've heard, there is space in the great trading halls. People's faces are set, their heads thrust forward, hurrying.

All the roads leading to the walled city of Troyes are guarded, for bandits are known to work the fair, stealing produce and coinage and anything else they can carry away. Other officials stand in the middle of the road, hands out to collect the toll for passing.

Father reaches into his pouch for the necessary fee.

"Good luck. May you prosper," says the toll keeper, a stout, friendly fellow. His good nature quickly vanishes when the next traveler, a poor tinker, cannot pay. Instantly the toll keeper seizes a sturdy club, which he swings menacingly, while the tinker retreats, groaning aloud.

On the road there is a constant clattering: the clapping of hooves; the racket of tin pots and pans, of beads and bells and buckets, as merchants and traders hurry toward the enormous city gate. Some have set up shop on the very roadside, unable to pay the rental for a stall or for a place in one of the great trading halls. A woman stands beside several cages with geese inside. Another is selling a cat,

shrieking out to all, "A fine mouser, this one! Only one-quarter denier!"

Of course, nobody will buy a cat, when bands of them roam over
the countryside and can be snatched up for free. The woman is obviously touched; but here, anyone can set up shop, even a crazy loon
or a foreigner or a Jew.

"Do we set up here?" I ask Father. I am breathless from excitement.

"No," Father replies. "We have rented a seat in the hall."

"The hall?" David exclaims, wide-eyed.

The hall! I feel like a prince. My very walk is different; the way
of a rich man.

Several Muslims squat at the side of the road: two men, a woman,
and three naked children. All are bone thin; and the children's eyes
look too round, too large. "This fine horse," says the one man, his
loins wrapped in dirty white cloth, and a shawl slung around his
thin neck. "For sale. You buy?" He slaps his hand against the bony
flank of a wretched-looking creature, black-and-white spotted, with
a smudge of brown on its ungainly head.

Father waves them aside.

I grasp Father's arm. "Maybe it is a good price," I say.

"At any price, it is too dear," says Father. "That creature looks
three-quarters on the way to its grave."

The horse has large feet, tufted with feathery hair, and a thin,
swishing tail. Flies settle around the horse's muzzle; it tolerates
them.

Boldly I approach the Muslim and ask, "What price?"

"Six denier," says the man, leaping up with astonishing agility.
"You want to take him now? A fine animal—eats very little."

David gives me a grin. "Hasn't eaten in a week, I'll wager," he
says. "Someone ought to take this poor creature and give it a meal."

"Come on," says Father, hurrying. "We must get to the hall and
claim our place—come on, you two! Enough foolishness."

I feel sudden longing. How Benjamin would love that wretched
old nag! If only I had some money, I could surely barter the Muslims
down to four, or even three, denier. Without money, one is lost, a

slave to duty, to rules. For the first time in my life, I crave money, almost as if I could breathe it, taste it, wear it like a shield. Money!

Once inside the enormous south gate, I see nothing but money— money changing hands, coins of silver and gold and mixed metal; money being passed, tossed, counted, stacked. People call out their wares—a tumult of voices rising and reverberating. "Fine glasses— the best—from Venice!" "Spices! Cinnamon and clove, pepper and cardamom, ginger!" Woven goods, embroideries! Enamel boxes! Little boxes! Charms! Charms against sickness, charms for love. Gold rings, silver chains, cloisonné, beautiful beads, feathers, flowers, stacks of fruit, handwoven baskets, urns of every size and shape. Fried cookies, crisp and sweet. Smoked eels and sardines and onion tarts—never could one see it all, hear it all, taste and touch it all. Never in a lifetime!

Inside the gate, we must pay another toll. The guard scrutinizes us. He peers into our cart. Grandfather is suddenly blooming with good spirits; his cheeks are pink. His eyes dart over the crowd, discover an old ally, and he shouts, "Ho! Abiru, where have you been, you old dog? Not since twenty years have I laid eyes on this man— this is my son and grandson. Upon my soul, you've not gotten any older."

The man rises from his squatting pose, his skin as tough and brown as the piles of leather beside him. He claps Grandfather on the back, kisses both his cheeks. "Do you know who else is here? That old Ari, from Constantinople. *Ach,* you can't imagine how he talks. Half the people of Constantinople have perished. Yes! It is a ghost town, thousands of people wiped out by a terrible pestilence. Thousands of bodies rotting in the streets. Ari is lucky he escaped. Haven't you heard?"

"We have heard rumors," says Father, shoulders hunched, face furrowed. "But surely it is a catastrophe limited to seaports and trading towns."

"Who can say?" replies Abiru. His dark face glistens with sweat, his mouth overflows with saliva as he relishes his tale. "Those afflicted spit blood. One day they are robust, two or three days later, their bodies swell and darken, and then they die. This pestilence is like no other. It takes the rich along with the poor. Children and parents, whole families . . ."

Suddenly I feel suffocated by the heat. Spitting blood? Bodies swelling up? I murmur, "Jacob told us about this same pestilence. He said it is in southern France. Will it come here? Does it travel?" Grandfather lays his hand on my shoulder. "Look, we have survived many catastrophes," he says. "The famine, when I was a child, the floods, the accusations of child murder. What can we do but go on day by day. It is all written, who shall live and who shall die."

Abiru nods rapidly and rasps, "Yes, it comes from putrid air. They say the Jews don't catch it because they are always bathing. Or is it that God watches over us? Who knows? I say we must be joyful. Eat and drink, dance a little."

"You look as if you've done more eating than dancing!" exclaims Grandfather, with a light punch to the man's belly. "We're off, we're off to the great hall."

"The great hall!" Abiru is impressed. "So, we small suckers sit outside; you barter in the great hall. Good luck! Good luck!"

Someone has to wait outside with the cart and the donkey and the goods. David volunteers. "Let Johannes go inside. Let him learn."

Now I forget all my fears, as I am carrying the skin bag full of coins, feeling many eyes upon me as we stride along the broad thoroughfare to the main square where the big business is done in the large guild halls. Street urchins and young maids, old men and farm women watch; and I am certain they are saying to themselves, "Look at that fine lad, already in business and barely grown—well, these Jews are clever in the ways of business, no denying that!" Proudly I enter the wide doorway, and, once inside, I am consumed by the noise and the air, heavy from the smell of many bodies pressed close and the eating of onions and garlic and spices, and, of course, the heat.

At one end of the hall the cloth merchants have displayed their wares, draped over baskets and tables, where the bookkeepers and money changers sit, and assistants take orders and promise delivery, and buyers shout out their specifications. "Now, it must be delivered to Flanders before winter, do you hear? We have to have time to make the cloth into robes, don't you know? Blue, that is the color they all want. Deep blue. You have it in quantity? Good, I pay you twenty percent down, the rest on delivery—what? You want forty now? You are insane!"

It goes on and on, until my hands are black from handling coins. It has taken hours to set up our stall. By the afternoon my eyes are smarting and my back aches, but there is a glorious feeling of being caught in a fast current, with everything moving around us and through us. Where would the world be without moneylenders? Without us Jews? How good it is to be at the center of things!

For a whole week, excepting on Sabbath, I am constantly working, making change, running to the other lenders to barter coins, copying down the names of debtors on my slate, along with the amount borrowed, interest due, the pledge given in trust. All this is done under Father's watchful eye. In the night, voices reverberate in my dreams; the din of coinage is constantly in my ears. I cannot loose myself from the trading. I am in constant terror of making a mistake, of being reproached by Father.

"Let the boy spend a day or so outside," says Grandfather. "He looks pale."

Father gives me a long look, then nods. "Tomorrow you and David can go around to sell the goods we brought: Frau Greta's cheeses and those bags of herbs from the butcher's daughter." Father gives me a wax tablet and a stylus. "You must keep their accounts with the utmost care," he says sternly, "and keep all their coins separately in these small bags. Never mix the money of others with your own."

I nod dutifully, though, of course, I know this. It is the first law of business not to mix funds and to keep careful records. I ask, "What of the armor and the other pledges: the mail shirt and the rings and other jewels. Shall we sell them, too?"

"Grandfather will sell the jewelry," says Father, and Grandfather's eyes shine, for he is still the most skilled at this. "You and David can take the visor and the mail shirt. It is not in the best shape, but see what you can do."

Father turns aside, dealing with a buyer of spices who needs funding for his journey east. Father will lend him the money for trans-

portation—for mule trains and ship passage and tolls. "I will pay
you back when I return and sell the spices. You will receive a per-
centage of the profit!" shouts the trader. As I watch, my eyes are
swimming, my heart pounding. How does Father know whom to
trust? How will I ever know? All this is like a mountain of debris
falling on my head. Outside the mimes are entertaining and someone is playing a recorder. I long to join them.

At last Father turns to me with a nod. "Go," he says. "You've been
a worthy helper."

My face feels flushed from this praise.

"Whatever money you make from selling the armor, and of course
the fee from the herbs, it shall be your own, as wages."

"Father! Thank you!" I would fling my arms around him, but this
is not what men do—especially not in the great hall. And anyhow,
I am no longer a child.

Outside, I cannot help but linger. Sugary cookies, almond-paste
candy, deep-fried crispy cakes all fill my senses. I do have some
coins in the small pouch at my waist, but they are not for filling my
belly. I have already seen a piece of red velvet cloth for Margarite.
It is a deep, pure, royal red, so beautiful that it will bring tears to
Margarite's eyes. Now I finger her small lace handkerchief and press
it to my nose.

Suddenly I feel a hand on my back. It is David, laughing and
gesturing at the dancers in the square, three young women in full
skirts, twirling and swaying, while two tall young men clap their
hands to the rhythm. The tune is new to me. I hold it in my thoughts,
singing bits of it until I have it firmly remembered. I take the flute
from my pocket and play along, and my notes join those of the man
with the recorder and the woman with the small gittern. The circle
widens to take me in.

Murmurs resound from the watching multitude, appreciative and
amazed. But other voices intrude. "Beware, the devil's tune," someone mutters. " 'Tis one of Satan's disguises to bring a merry song
and lead good Christians to temptation."

"*Uch,* it's only a boy playing for the love of it, can't you see?"

"I see his evil gleam, I do, and I will not be taken in!"

David touches my arm. "Let us go," he says. "Have you seen the glassblower? The shoemaker? Beautiful wares, I tell you; embroideries, vessels of copper and gold."

I lead David to a textile dealer and show him the red velvet cloth I want to buy for Margarite. "Buy it now!" exclaims David. He fingers the cloth, approving my choice; and in a twinkling it is done, the cloth is folded and tied. I tuck it under my shirt and David says, "Let us go now and sell those cheeses."

I have a bold idea. "Why not take them to the hostel or a tavern? They need much food and may pay a higher price than we can get outside the gate from a passing farmer."

"Well done!" We hasten to the back door of the first tavern, called the Six Silver Spoons. The owner, a large woman with only three teeth in her mouth and a black mole on her cheek, pulls us inside and examines the cheeses, shaking her head, clucking and breathing hard from her labors. "What price?"

I name an outrageous price, as such things are done. The woman slashes it in half. I raise. She cuts.

"Of course," I say cannily, "if you should purchase all of them, the price could be lowered." I name a good price. Frau Greta would be overjoyed. And one-tenth of it will go to my family, payment for making the trade. I am scarcely breathing.

The woman fixes me with a steely stare.

I stand firm, unblinking.

"Done, then," says the woman, taking charge of the cheeses by enfolding them in her ample arms. "Is this all you have?" she asks.

"It's all we have this time, Good Mother," I tell her. "Next year we can bring you double, if you like."

She sniffs, wipes her nose with the back of her hand. "Who knows what will be next year? We could all be in our graves."

"The bargain is fulfilled only on condition that you are alive," I say.

The woman bursts out laughing; David and I laugh, too. "You are a strange fellow." She chuckles. "Your sort are usually so solemn. I did not know that Jews could laugh."

"I have also some powerful healing herbs," I say, feeling bold. I take the herbs from my satchel. The small bags are tied with dainty lavender ribbon. "Perchance you could use something for headache or sleeplessness?"

The woman squints. "How much?"

I give her the price. "Special," I add, smiling, "for you."

"I will take one," she says, "in exchange for two glasses of ale."

"The herbs are not ours," I protest.

"What business is it of mine?" counters the woman. "You pay your sweetheart back for the herbs, I give you the ale, we are all even."

I am dumbfounded.

David speaks up. "How do you know they come from his sweetheart?"

The woman laughs heartily as she leads us inside and pours out the ale. "It is written all over his face," she says. "Especially in the eyes."

She pours ale into our cups to the very brim, foaming. Never have I tasted ale so sweet, so pure. "Sit," says the woman, nodding to a bench. And there we sit, David and I, drinking ale with the best of them in a tavern at Troyes! I feel the bubbles in my head. I want to laugh and laugh, and I drum a song onto the tabletop with my fingers. A young serving girl comes by with a pitcher and fills our cups once again. As she bends down, I see the soft flesh of her upper arms and the glow of sweat on her lip. Curls creep out beneath the ruffle of her cap. I sigh with pleasure, and I turn to David. "Aren't women beautiful?"

"Indeed," answers my uncle. "They are."

From the other end of the tavern comes a roar of laughter, as five men and two women engage in jokes and stories. Their tall cups of mead are overflowing, and a rack of pork is being brought to the table, along with huge trenchers of bread and a roasted duck.

A workman sitting on a bench beside David gives him a poke. "Italians," he says with a wry look. "Spending money like there was no tomorrow. Drinks for everybody! They've been here for three days, living like kings."

"They are lords?" asks David. "Traders, perhaps in spices?"

The man laughs, throwing his head back, so that rotting teeth show in his wide open mouth. "Revelers, they are. Running from the pestilence. Left their towns, their homes, their wives, and little ones. They were over a dozen men at the outset. Now only five remain; the others died soon after departing. Eat, drink, and be merry, for tomorrow we are dead men!"

"We have heard about this pestilence," says David. "And these men have *seen* it! What do they say can be done?"

"Some say that breathing putrid air is a remedy against it; they hover over the latrine and breathe in the stink."

I look at David, my hand clapped over my mouth.

"Others say to take a small bottle of herbs and spices and hold it to the nose when walking about. It wards off the evil vapors." The man laughs. "I rather favor this method, wouldn't you?"

David fingers his beard, deep in thought. "Packets of herbs and spices, is it?"

"Truly!" I give a shout. "Then one would do well to purchase these!"

David and I exchange a look. In accord, we move closer to the rowdy group, sitting down at the table beside theirs. The smell of roast duck is almost overpowering. The men and women are raising the roof with their noise, interrupting each other, gesturing broadly, knocking over chairs. Nobody can understand their words, but their gestures are clear. A false exuberance rings out, an air of total abandon.

A slender, pale-faced priest, sitting under the eaves, apparently knows their language. The priest translates for the gentleman beside him, who tells it to his companion, who repeats it loudly for any and all listeners. Soon the whole tavern strains and rocks and reacts to the horrors.

"All in a single day, I tell you, so many they had not space in the cemetery but had to make enlargement of it. Finally they just set the bodies ablaze right there in the street. You can imagine the stink of burning flesh, and rotted, too, from the pestilence—did you know they turn black?"

"Why, I know families that took their children and threw them on the dead-cart, still alive, just wanting to get them out of the house!"

"In Milan there were these four families, all infested. The local council took it in hand. They boarded up the houses and set them on fire."

"Did it stop the spread of the disease?"

"Not likely. It spread everywhere. It's come to Avignon, you know. Even His Holiness the Pope is terrified."

A strange silence descends.

"Listen now!" the priest calls out. A tavern can be a church in a manner of speaking, so say his posture and his tone. He extends his arms. "Pray, brothers! Give to charity. The church is receiving alms now, promises, stipends. It might not be too late."

"Immoderate living no doubt spreads the sickness," says a woman, eating a leg of mutton. "One must take care, remain pure in one's habits," says her companion, as she consumes a plateful of cabbage and pork.

"Oh, you can talk all you will about natural calamities; earthquakes and volcanoes and evil humors, they say, led to this pestilence," says the priest, expanding his audience. "Nothing happens except as God wills it. That is the truth. And these men cannot escape the wrath of God, except by giving charity and doing penance." The priest nods toward the table, where the group is now tearing into the duck, tossing small bones over their shoulders, pounding on the table for more beer.

I feel myself shrinking into the shadows, and David, too, sits stock-still, afraid to be noticed, unwilling to make a sound or a move. But then I reach into my satchel for a packet of herbs and signal to David. He nods.

"We have here a packet of healing herbs," David says loudly. With exaggerated gestures he opens the small bag, takes out a pinch of the stuff, and rolls it between his fingers. "Pungent and pure," he says, a little louder, "grown in the fields of Strasbourg by an innocent virgin." He pauses, inhales the herbs, breathes out grandly. "They say that these herbs and spices purify the air all around, cleansing the impure vapors that bring disease."

An elderly man with but one eye starts toward David, hand outstretched. "What are you asking for these packets?"

"I'm not sure, sir, that I have enough to go around to all who want them," says David. "How many have we, Johannes?"

"Only twenty," I say, holding the satchel shut, "but ten of them are promised already to the wool merchants in the great hall. We were just about to go and deliver them."

Now all eyes are upon us. These people believe that all Jews are healers and magicians, that we know secret incantations and charms with the power not only to work mischief but also to work cures. Our Jew hats have become objects of fascination and of hope.

One man leans over and smacks three florins down upon the table in front of me. His friend gasps. "Are you mad, Berno? That is a small fortune!"

The first man responds, "What are three florins in exchange for one's health?"

The price has been fixed. Now I am lost in the excitement of barter, coins ringing, hands stretching and grasping, glad praises. "These Jews are right clever. They know mysteries. Taught by the devil, perhaps, but still it can help us in need."

"Yes, yes. One of our town Jews set this arm for me when the bones broke. Good as new, though they are sorcerers. They must be watched, 'tis true."

David gathers all the coins and stuffs them into his leather bag, while I dispense the herb packets. Then swiftly we rise and hurry out to the lanes, knowing that in only a matter of minutes the mood could change and we would be in serious danger.

CHAPTER
ELEVEN

S ome afternoons David and I take time to go to Cathedral Square, where we stand and watch the plays being performed. One afternoon, with the sun bright and hot, we join the crowd to watch a play about a seafaring man and his wife, a sharp-tongued crone who bests him at every turn. She burns the meat, waves her fist, smashes the plate, beats him with a stick. We roar with laughter. The wife, at the end, is overcome with remorse when the husband brings home a sack of gold (a sack of leaves is used for the play). She falls on her knees, begs his pardon, kisses his boot. But, alas, the seaman has found another—a dainty young maiden, docile and sweet. The audience is delighted. Justice has been done, and everyone has given vent to many feelings.

We will try to sell the armor this afternoon. After this entertainment, there will surely be lighthearted buyers ready to make a purchase that signifies romance and valor.

"Put on the mail coat," suggests David. "Show how it gleams. Put on the visor—so. How fine you look, Johannes!"

With the mail coat on my chest, I feel transformed into a bold warrior. I feel brilliant, I feel powerful. I understand now why they make us wear the Jew hat. Pointed and cheap and ridiculous, it is meant to rob us of our pride. The hat does not belong with the mail coat; I stuff it inside my tunic and don the visor instead.

David and I stroll among the pleasure seekers, and David calls out, "For sale, this visor and mail coat—solid and true—see the workmanship! Name your price. We can sell separately the visor and mail coat, if you will, or all together. Name your price."

Three young men stride up to us. Desire is plain in their eyes, though they try to disguise it with their swagger. "I will give you six silver coins for the mail coat—though I see it is badly frayed in places."

"By your leave, my lord," I reply smoothly, "this restoration is perfect. My grandfather, a workman of great skill, has taken it into his hands. The coat is worth at least twelve florin, but today . . ."

I feel sweat running down my sides. The moment of conquest is near. This day is nearly done; soon the Angelus will ring, merchants will close their stalls for the day, and all will retire to the taverns, the inns, the outlying fields. I am burning to make the sale.

"See the pattern, the reinforcement here at the breast and back." I turn around to let them look. I set the mask down over my face. They gasp admiringly. There is talk among the three, murmuring, arguing; and then they seem ready, like ripe fruit.

But something shifts. Is there a sudden chill breeze, to make leaves scatter and heads turn? People hurry to the city wall. Watchmen call out from the ramparts. A distant noise, like wind, grows louder, then louder still. It is the sound of low chanting and the shuffling of feet, mingled now with the flurries of talk bursting all around, until people are shouting. "Flagellants! Flagellants come to give us a show! Ho, now, see this, see this."

"Come away," cries David, but it is too late. The crowd has submersed us. Pushing and moving like a great beast, it brings us along, so that David with his Jew hat and I with my mail coat and visor become one with the unfolding spectacle.

A procession is coming, steadily and relentlessly moving near, like a glacier or an avalanche. A mass of moving shapes clad in white from cowl to toe, the men and women march toward the crowd. Blazing red crosses on their chests and backs attest to their purpose. They are soldiers of Christ, marching for survival.

Church bells ring; several priests rush to join the holy throng that, by its march and by its penance, will banish sickness and pestilence. The flagellants will beat themselves until they bleed. They will offer to Christ their prayers for forgiveness. Their self-inflicted punishment is to be their cost for staying alive.

Two by two they come, steady in their pace, silent, then erupting into song, a mournful dirge. I feel the hair rising on the back of my neck as their song resonates. I will flee! I turn, but I am imprisoned by the throng of watchers who press upon me from all sides. Terror surrounds me, makes it difficult to breathe. I feel the lust of the crowd, their sudden camaraderie, the heat of their bodies, the smell of their sweat. Now the shouts rise around me, beating against my face. "Flagellants! Flagellants!"

The flagellants proceed, relentless in their march. Their leader bears a banner of purple velvet and gold. The gold shimmers in the late afternoon sun, giving off a brilliant otherworldly reflection. The crowd gasps, as if this were truly a sign from Heaven—approval for what will yet transpire.

The hooded brothers and sisters of the cross now enter the city gates, passing through the streets, past the stalls, and to the central marketplace. Everyone is touched by their coming. Everything else ceases. The purpose is noble: to win God's approval and forgiveness, to stem the pestilence, and to rid the land of sin and unhealthy emanations.

The marchers form a large circle—some two hundred—of a single voice and single will. To endure. To suffer. To avert the horrible death that stalks Europe. Their leader speaks, softly at first, then raging. All eyes follow his every move. Bodies strain toward him. He is magnificent in his wrath.

"The pestilence we have seen—the curses we have witnessed— defy description." He goes on to describe the families destroyed in a single day, their carcasses piled high; he tells of houses burned down with the living yet inside. He tells of bandits preying upon the sick and survivors alike, looting and raping. "It is so in Florence, in Milan, in Marseilles, and in Lorraine—the horror creeps nearer every day. A few escape into churches. It helps them not. Priests die, and nuns and bishops—the reverent along with the wicked, the rich along with the poor. Like fire the pestilence creeps and leaps and rages. And it is coming here. Brothers! Sisters! It is also coming here."

The crowd is milling now, aghast, terrified. What can be done?

The flagellants begin their grotesque dance. Faster, faster, and now they raise their whips behind them—thick, knotted leather thongs tipped with iron spikes. Cries blare from the audience as the blows fall, blows hurled backward with such vigor that blood spurts when the spike hits flesh. Women of the town rush up, screaming, to catch the sacred blood in a cloth and smear it upon their foreheads, their eyes, their mouths. The women wail for mercy. Mercy! I have never imagined such a sight. All control is gone now; they have seen blood.

"Come away!" David pulls at my arm, but we are powerless, held in by the throng and their passion. They are wild, crazy, drunk. David shouts, "Come away! Run, Johannes!"

But we are trapped, and all around us the frenzy grows, like a spreading flame. The leader shouts encouragement to the beaters, and exhortations to the crowd, "There have been confessions . . . Yea, we must drive them out . . . instruments of God's vengeance, some have dabbled in black arts, in treachery, spreading poison."

Someone is spreading poison, bringing the pestilence—someone.

The leader stands in the midst of the writhing, bleeding penitents, shouting, "They spread—like those lepers did years ago! Did you know they tried to poison the entire land? And did you know they were helped by the Jews?"

Ah, now it is out—the word, the tainted name. *Jew*. The cry is taken up by many voices all around us. "The Jews! The Jews!"

"Killers and poisoners—they drink the blood of our children, they desecrate the host, they poison the water—"

"The Jews! They *conspire* against us." The chant rises; the dreaded word flies like a stone thrown into the crowd. "*Conspired* to kill our Lord, they *conspire* to kill our children, *conspire* to pollute our faith, our air, the very water that we drink—"

And suddenly I am blinded. Bodies fall over me, on top of me. My bones feel crushed. The metal of the mail coat is cutting into my flesh. The visor presses down on my skull. I feel suffocated, floating, beyond terror, my only gasping need is for air. Air!

Suddenly, there is air again, and brightness from the sky as the last bursts of sunlight suffuse the earth. It is like the end of the world, the end of time. Shouts still resound in my ears, but they are dim, echoing. The march has altered its course, and the mob is in pursuit. And I lie there on the ground, watching. I am neither pursued nor pursuer—I am like an invisible creature, eyes and ears overfull with evil.

The mob finds weapons—sticks, rocks, knives, hooks, hammers, and cudgels—screaming, *"There's one! The pointed cap, the money bag, the hair . . . Jew! Jew!"* and *"Look, the badge, the Jew badge; and there's a Muslim—get him!"*

People try to flee, protesting. It is useless. The mob has its own pulse, seeks its own prey. It crashes into stalls, rushes over the cart that belongs to poor Abiru, and in a moment that man is down, crushed like an insect beneath a thousand stamping feet. In an instant the stack of hides is looted. Goods vanish from stalls. Animals are turned loose or abducted or killed.

Where are the magistrates? The bailiff at the gate? The guards who stand atop the city wall to keep order?

"David!" I scream out. "David!" I cannot find David. He has vanished.

In the melee I glimpse parts of bodies—a grin, then a grimace of sheer hatred such as seems incredible by man toward man. *Why do they hate us? Why do they hate me?*

I run through an opening in the crowd, realizing now that I am thoroughly disguised by the mail coat. For a moment my soul rises. Then I feel utterly alone. *Father. Grandfather. David.*

I dash in and out of lanes, behind buildings, searching for David. I cannot escape the roar of the crowd, the flames that burst up from sudden fires. I hear crashing and splintering sounds of objects—or bones—being broken.

And then, somehow, the thing expires. A strange stillness settles over the town, reaching out to the fields, where not even the birds or the beasts are stirring. I move as if through a mist, my body aching. The ache comes from within, a deep, burning pit. How can such things happen? I know nothing, my mind is fastened on only one word: *David.*

Somehow Father finds me; he staggers toward me, like an apparition. His arms enfold me. I feel his tears on my face.

"You're safe!" He pummels me, pulls me close yet again, his large hands holding, grasping, caressing me. "Why did you go into that crowd? What are you doing in that armor? Where is David? My God! My God, I thought you were dead."

I cannot breathe. All the past moments of terror are collected now in my chest and throat. Finally I gasp: "David—lost—they caught him, I think. I couldn't . . . do . . . anything. Where is . . . Grandfather?"

"We hid in the abbey. They hid us. Some nuns. Grandfather is still there, waiting." Sweat covers Father's face, though the night air is clammy and cold. "Come. We must find Uncle David," he says in a tone devoid of hope.

And at last we do find him lying in a cart filled with firewood, the cart turned on its side. At first we do not know who it is, or even that it is a man; perhaps a twisted stump, something unrecognizable. Then, at once, we both know. There is no breath in my body, no feeling in my hands as I look upon this horror.

A moan, very low, hisses from David's lips, which are puffed and bloody. A small curl of blood seeps from the side of his mouth. His shirt is torn at the breast, where he has been pierced. Both feet and both hands bear testament to the effort the mob has made upon David to bring revenge for the body of another so pierced, then crucified. It is not a new tactic. Year after year, again and again, the mob finds a target upon which to reenact the Passion.

Father bends down. I bring my face near to David's. If only my breath could heal! If only my love could soothe! David opens his eyes. The lids flutter slightly. He murmurs, "Thank God. We are—"

"We will use the cart," says Father, leaping up now, as if a sudden strength would turn him into a giant. He tosses the wood from the cart, rights it again with a single mighty heave. "Into the cart!" A pool of blood remains where David has lain. It is dark in color, congealing. And now as the dawn comes, I see that David's face is pale, pale as the morning moon.

For three days David lingers in the nether room of the abbey. It is a cold place—a place for prisoners or fugitives or the insane—but it is sheltered; and the nuns are kind to let us stay. David lies on a bed of straw on the floor of packed mud. Hollows in the stone wall create cavelike spaces, where the dampness lingers. In a niche, I discover a long leg bone and several smaller bones. I do not tell Father and Grandfather about the bones.

Father and Grandfather venture out to look for a physician. They come back alone, and report on the carnage and the destruction. But the fair goes on, the daily barter is little affected by what happened. Some have asked for Menachem the Jew—why isn't he at his post? Father and Grandfather and I sit and stare out at nothing. We listen to David's breathing, and we pray. Father sends me to the kitchen of the convent to buy food—a few eggs, some almonds, milk. David sips the milk. Otherwise, he will not eat. I find one last packet of Margarite's herbs. With two stones, I grind them to a powder and put them into the milk. They do not bring any strength to David, who lies staring at the craggy ceiling, eyes open whether awake or sleeping.

The second day, two nuns stand at the open doorway of the cellar. One carries a candle, though it is daylight. The older nun is tall and gaunt. Years of service and devotion have cut deep lines and furrows into her face.

The younger, obviously a novitiate, is a plump girl with sturdy peasant limbs and jowls. She enters smiling, bending toward the sick man. She straightens, whispers to the elder Sister, "But—where are his horns?"

The other replies softly, with some disdain, "They are retracted, of course, like the claws of a cat. Don't ask foolish questions, Sister Augustine, we are here to save him." Her gaze lingers a moment on David's sagging form. "Perhaps some blood should be let."

Grandfather grunts. "He is half dead from lack of blood."

"Still, we have found it beneficial, together with prayers, of course," she says.

I look at David. His eyes are wide open now. Through parched lips he moans. "No prayers."

"If you would but accept our Savior," cries the younger, Sister Augustine, "surely a miracle of healing could occur! We will pray for you," she says eagerly, "in Jesu's name."

"No." It is a harsh whisper. David lifts his head. His voice gains strength. "If I did this thing," he says, "and I lived by it, what would I say on the day of my death? That I betrayed my Lord?"

"Come, Sister," says the elder. "They are a stubborn lot, as I told you, but we have done our duty in the attempt. Would that they could see the truth! But they are blinded by their allegiance to Satan."

When the nuns leave, David waves his hand, summoning me to draw near. "Don't be afraid, Johannes," he whispers. "I have—I have loved."

I wait to hear more, but David's eyes become clouded, and he lies back, his breathing shallow.

The third day, David half rises. "Play for me, Johannes!" he calls out.

I am awakened from a deep sleep filled with terrible dreams. I start up, running. "What?"

"The wedding song—remember? The song of the bride and groom. Play for me, Johannes!"

Only four years ago I, with the other musicians, played that song as David was brought to his bride in the flower-filled room, where she sat radiant and beautiful. Tamara. I learned the song especially for the wedding. It is a beautiful, beautiful song.

Now I bring the flute to my lips, and I play, remembering the words.

> *Sing to the groom,*
> *Oh, happy hearts,*
> *Sing to the bride and groom*
> *For as he comes, so too shall* he
> *For whom we've waited long.*

> *Let flowers bloom*
> *And birds make song*
> *Play with harp and lyre*
> *The blessings sung, the bells are rung*
> *And every soul on fire.*

The flames of love
Are burning bright
The groom beholds the bride
As blessings flow down from above
He rushes to her side.

Oh, joyous groom
Oh, happy bride
May you live well and long
May faith abound with children round
In love's eternal bond.

"Again," whispers David through parched lips. Again I play, and again, and yet again. The happy tune lifts from my flute, while my heart is breaking.

In the chaos, the donkey vanished. Perhaps it, too, is dead.

Father and Grandfather and I confer. The death of David has created a new harmony among us. We are more than relatives. We are three men, equal in grief, and none of us asks the question: How can we possibly go home without David? How can we explain it to the women, who will surely hold us accountable? Grief always seeks answers, although none are ever found.

Somehow I know that I must lead, as if Father and Grandfather have suddenly grown old and incapable. I propose a plan. They agree. We pick up our possessions, the bag of money, the strongbox, the few pledges that were not stolen in the melee. At least the money is safe, for Father fled with it to the abbey when the riot began. Oh, how dearly the Jews love their money, accusers will taunt us, as though we are the only ones who realize that without money one is as good as dead.

Nearby the city gates the Muslims still wait with their dull-coated nag. The woman and children are not to be seen; perhaps they have gone begging, and who could blame them? I step up to the man with the rags over his loins, and within less time than it takes to drink a cup of ale, the bargain is proposed and sealed. The Muslim rushes off, hands raised heavenward and shouting. I take the horse by its tattered reins and lead it back to the abbey, where Father and Grandfather wait beside Uncle David's body, now stiff and hard.

Together the three of us hoist his body over the horse. It is done with great difficulty. I can only bear it if I think of nothing at all, but that is impossible, so I think of Benjamin, and how he will cry out for joy when he sees this horse as his own.

CHAPTER
TWELVE

I dreamed of incredible things, of great palaces of joy, where people are shown wonders, then put to death. In that place, people chose their death, the way one chooses a path through the woods. Why would anybody choose death? What can it mean?

Surely David did not want to die. I think of the two nuns and their offer. They have no idea what it is to be a Jew, to vow partnership with the God of Abraham. The partnership is like a marriage, forsaking all others and lasting forever. I know now that this is what David meant when he asked me, again and again, to play the wedding song.

With the first light every morning, I feel that thud of pain again—a fist in my stomach: David is dead. Never again will I see him, or laugh or make music with him.

Homeward bound, we do not speak much. Grandfather sits on the horse, moving from side to side with the animal's slow, plodding gait. Father listlessly walks alongside. I lead the way home.

There is nothing to say, nothing to discuss. I am flooded with memories, not only of David but of my childhood. This journey seems to be a turning point in my life. I leave childhood behind. And my memories, now, hold special meaning.

I recall seeing the man with the baby on the bridge. I remember playing with Gunther and Jacob when we were all small boys. I used to play "Crusader," until Father pulled me aside and explained that, years ago, knights went on crusades to conquer the "infidels"— that is, to get the Holy Land back from the Muslims—and on the way, the knights practiced their killing skills on lepers and Jews.

"It is not right for a Jewish lad to play at crusading," Father said. I am ashamed of the times I tried on the armor, wanting to become someone else. God, too, knows my wickedness. But then, were it not for the coat of mail and the visor, I could very well be dead. Perhaps it was God's will for me to don that armor the very hour that the flagellants came. Then, if God has saved me, it must be for a purpose. Why did He take David and allow me to live?

As we trudge on toward home, I wonder how we will live the rest of our lives. Will anything ever be beautiful again? Remarkably, as we reach the edge of the forest, then the river, I feel a rush of gratitude and amazement. Our steps quicken. Even the horse comes alive. Its head bobs and its feet lift a little higher. Grandfather sits up straight. How very far we have been! How very dear is this place, its nodding trees, the summer blossoms, the half-timbered houses with their steeply inclined roofs, the low fences with chickens and pigs and cattle inside—everything seems unbearably beautiful.

As we approach the city gates, as if on signal, church bells ring out. Usually, for the Jews, the bells are a nuisance and a loathsome reminder that we are outsiders. Today the bells ring welcome; we are home. I am suddenly ravenous. Then with abrupt force comes the awful knowledge, like a hammer blow: David.

In Mother's face, the moment she comes to the door, I see that she has guessed it, denied it, absorbed it.

"Where is David?" she asks, in a quavering voice. "Where is he?"

Grandfather slumps, mute, upon the horse.

Father moves toward Mother, both hands outstretched. In ordinary times they do not touch in the presence of others, for the sake of modesty. Now Father clasps her hands. Their words tangle together like knotted threads, each asking, answering, attempting to understand the impossible

"David? Where is David?"

"The flagellants . . ."

"Why is Grandfather on that horse?"

"Abraham, is it you? Thank God you are home safe."

"Grandmother hasn't been well. She worried so."

"We buried him in the town—it was great trouble."

"Three days. David was with us for three days."

"David refused their prayers."

"Johannes played for him, and then . . ."

After all the questions are asked and answered, it starts again—the same questions, the same answers. Still nothing is clear. It happens to everyone, and yet it seems impossible to be here one day and not here the next, to leave on a journey and simply not return.

Neighbors come. How do they know? Some undercurrent travels, like a silent river, from house to house, carrying the awful news. We sit on the floor, in mourning. People speak softly, or not at all. Do not attempt to comfort the mourner when his dead lie before him, say the sages.

Neighbors bring food: salted fish, smoked meat, boiled eggs, and fresh bread. Someone brings a dish of cooked lentils. The food is set out on platters on the large wooden table. Nobody feels like eating, really, but somehow the food disappears; hunger is always grief's companion.

Dovie, the shipbuilder; Zemel, the baker; Frau Freda; Moshe the Bent; Elias, the butcher; Saul, the gardener; the *shochet*; the tailor; the bathhouse keeper—all appear with their spouses and their little ones.

I am surrounded by the faces of my people, the community I have known all my life. Every face is distinct and dear. Jacob is there, and Margarite, and her parents and her sister. Rochele and Rosa find each other and whisper together in the secret way of little girls. They are solemn; their hair shines. I see Margarite gazing at them, and in the next moment we are standing together, looking into each other's eyes.

"Johannes, I am so sorry . . ."

"It is so good to be home."

"It seemed like such a long time."

"I have much to tell you. We must talk, Margarite. About us. Our future." I hear these bold words of mine, and I am astonished but also unabashed. I must speak for myself now. I am fully a man.

"Perhaps you will visit us when your *shivah* is over," she says.

"I will surely do so," I say. "I have your money from the herbs."

"Do not speak of it now. Later will suffice," she says, smiling.

I see Margarite's beauty, but there is more. I notice how much taller I am than she, and I am filled with the desire to shield her. Then, too, there is that other desire, to know her caring and her warmth. I need her. The world is too bitter without one's own special love.

In her hands Margarite holds a carved box. "I have brought some herbs," she says, "for your grandmother, may she regain her health soon."

"Her legs are sorely swollen," I say, nodding sadly. "She cannot walk."

"We will pray for her healing," says Margarite.

The two little girls approach, and I say playfully to Rosa, "Tell your sister that I bought her a gift at the fair. A cloth of red velvet. Perchance she will make a cloak of it. Unless," I add, "your sister is not one for sitting around and sewing."

Margarite flashes a smile. She turns to Rochele. "Tell your brother that I will gladly sew," she says. "And perhaps there is enough cloth also to make a vest. Does your brother wear a vest?"

The little girls giggle softly.

I feel the strangeness of it—joy in the midst of sorrow, sorrow in the midst of joy. It has always been so for us. At the height of the joyful wedding feast, the groom will crush a glass under his foot to signify the loss of the holy temple and to show that joy and sorrow cohabit always, for we are not yet in Heaven.

Soon the reality of life in Strasbourg returns. While I was away, I imagined that nothing had changed during my absence. But everything changes; we are only too close to see it happening day by day. Rochele is suddenly taller and more excitable. Benjamin studies constantly for his bar mitzvah. He reads the sacred texts with Rabbi Meier and Meier's sons, studying by candlelight. Grandmother does not move from her pallet the whole day long. Grandfather bends to hear her voice; and when he moves away, he has great difficulty pulling himself upright again.

Father and I pay calls on our debtors—noblemen, monks, and

priests are among them. I stand by, watching, and now I interject, speaking to the debtors for the first time in my father's presence. "Sir, we must collect our interest. It is our livelihood."

"Yes, yes," says Baron Zims, who has hounds and horses and loves carnivals and tournaments. "We also have our expenses. You must be patient."

Father takes up the argument. "You agreed to the interest. We have your signed agreement."

"I agreed under the force of circumstances," says the baron. "The interest is much too high, and you know it."

"We also have expenses," says Father, "taxes to pay, a family to feed."

"You Jews are always complaining," snorts the baron. "You would do well to learn to live among us with less hostility."

I see Father's pain in the way he walks, the way his hands are limp at his sides. I say, "Why must we be moneylenders? Why must we live here?"

"We are moneylenders because there is no other work for us. We have always lived in Strasbourg, since Grandfather was a boy."

"But why must we be treated like stray dogs? We pay our taxes. We do our duty. Are we not citizens, too?"

"No, we are not!" He speaks angrily. "Where else should we go? We have no country. We are not Germans or French or Italians. We are Jews and only Jews."

I want to argue and shout, I want to ask questions. Suppose that more gentiles were moneylenders? Suppose they no longer need us at all—what then? But I remain silent, feeling an unreasoning anger at my poor father, who is so downcast.

I go alone to Frau Greta the Winker, to take the proceeds from her cheeses. She pokes her head out the door at my knock, as if to bar some animal inside from escaping. Greta edges herself out the door, her face bright with expectation.

But from inside comes a guttural cry. "You would leave me here to rot in the darkness, you witch! Never let me see your hideous face again!"

I brace myself against the shouting. "Open the door! Give me some air for a change, instead of this foul stink from your pottage and your slimy bed."

Gently Greta closes the door behind her, emerging solemn, her brow knotted. "He is not well," she says softly, inclining her head back toward the house. "My husband."

"I am sorry to hear it," I say mildly.

"Well, it is not a new story. Everyone knows what they did to him."

I do not know, exactly, nor do I want to ask. I give Greta the sack of coins, a goodly weight. Greta makes a cry of astonishment, seizes the sack and peers inside, then clutches the sack to her breast. "Thank you, thank you. Now we shall eat. Now we can live."

"Next year," I tell her, "God willing, we will sell many more for you. I met an innkeeper who ordered three times as many."

"Christ be praised!" Greta cries out, glancing heavenward. She leans toward me with breathless pride. "My son, Gunther, he is now in a position with the city council. They pay him to keep the place clean, the chambers and the streets outside. They gave him a special cap to wear. He is bringing in some money, too."

"Very nice," I say. "Congratulations."

Another roar comes from inside the house. "Greta! Greta!"

"I must go." Greta winks her apology, as she slides through the doorway to be engulfed in curses.

Benjamin and I revisit Herr Closener, bringing him a return letter from the monk in Troyes. Benjamin brings the horse along, insisting that it needs the exercise. In just this past week, that horse has been brushed a hundred times, its hooves washed, mane combed and braided. "Are you planning to clean its teeth?" I ask as we walk along, Benjamin leading the horse by a rope.

"Do you think it is necessary?" Benjamin asks, unaware of my mirth. He pulls up the horse's lip, peers at the yellow teeth. "Perhaps with cloves? What do you think?"

"I think you are nursemaid to a horse." I laugh heartily. Benjamin gives me a punch and a grin.

Fritsche Closener welcomes us kindly. The hound sniffs at Benjamin's shoes.

"We have a horse!" Benjamin bursts out.

"Fine-looking animal," says Closener, giving me a secret wink. "I can see he will flourish under your care."

"Daily my brother takes him up to the hills where the grass is tender," I say.

"Some animals are treated better than people," says the scribe. "You have brought me a letter? Thank you, thank you." He takes two silver coins from his waistband, hands one to each of us.

"Oh, we don't expect pay," Benjamin objects.

I want to stop up his mouth! I only stand there, helpless.

"I insist," says Closener. "One must pay his debts, and I owe you for the service. A trustworthy messenger is worth his weight in gold!"

We take the coins and bid farewell. At the door Herr Closener tells me, "Don't forget, we want to make some music together. Perhaps you learned a new tune at the fair."

"That I did," I say. Then I tell him, "We lost my uncle David at the fair."

Herr Closener nods. "I heard. I am sorry. I did not want to speak of it, in case . . . it seemed . . ." The scribe waves his hand for want of proper words.

"Thank you," I say, knowing the gulf that separates us, making it difficult to speak of matters too private, for we do not know each other's ways.

"*Grüss Gott,*" says Herr Closener, in parting.

"*Grüss Gott.*" May God greet you.

Benjamin hoists himself onto the horse.

"Have you named him?" I ask.

"Her. 'Tis a mare, can't you tell?"

"What's her name, then?"

"Matilda," Benjamin says instantly. "I love that name, don't you?"

Before I can answer, I see three magistrates hurrying toward the house of Meister Jakon, the singer. One carries a stout truncheon. Another holds a length of chain slung over his shoulder. I know these three: They are the lackeys of noblemen like Zorn and

Engelbracht, and men who sit on the city council. The lackeys have their own way of walking, lurching from side to side. They wear leather breeches and pointed shoes and cloaks with leather patches. Their hats are pulled over their foreheads, nearly covering their eyes.

Benjamin and I stop dead in our tracks. We would make ourselves blend into the shrubbery if we could. I motion to Benjamin, who dismounts and examines one of the horse's hooves with utmost concentration. "Caught a stone, did he?" I say loudly.

The officials are pounding on the door. Meister Jakon emerges, blinking at the sunlight, his hair rumpled, as if from sleep. "Yes? What is it, please?"

"What is it, please?" mimics the magistrate holding the truncheon behind his back. "You are wanted for questioning, Meister Jakon. You have been named in an inquiry."

"But I . . . but I know nothing—what is this about?"

"You will know soon enough. Come."

"Wait! Let me get my—"

"Everything you need will be taken care of," says the one with the chain.

"You'll be back home before dark," says the other.

"It is only a formality," says the one with the truncheon.

Reluctantly, my heart pounding, I steal a glance at the group. Two of the officials now grasp the singer's arms, and they pull him quickly along the road. For an instant I see Meister Jakon's eyes, the terror in them. Meister Jakon opens his mouth, as if to call out. Quickly he closes it again, and they pass by.

The community seethes with the news. Hardly has one shock been digested when another occurs. People gather in the streets, by the well; they stop work in their stalls and gardens, and speak together. "What did he do? Meister Jakon, the singer? Did you hear he has been arrested?"

"Who knows? They took him for questioning. His wife is frantic with worry. She goes to the prison, but they won't tell her anything."

Before Sabbath services, Rabbi Meier stands outside in the courtyard, gathering everyone in with his words. "All will be well. It is some mistake," says the rabbi. "We will pray for our brother."

"We should form a committee," says Vivelin, the wealthy moneylender, "and request of the council that they at least tell us the charges."

" 'Committee.' " Reb Zebulon, the teacher, ponders this. "When did it ever help us to send a committee? They refuse to acknowledge us."

"If we behave as if we have no power," retorts Vivelin, "then we will be treated like serfs. We are free men here! We all do business in the town. We pay our taxes."

The men look at one another. The women shake their heads and draw their children close. "Come," says the rabbi. "The Sabbath queen is about to arrive."

The sun has set. Sabbath is here. No sorrow or strife must intrude. Inside the synagogue I sit with Benjamin and Jacob, behind Father and several of the older men. Grandfather, his joints aching, has stayed home. The prayers and chants and songs surround me, bringing that elevated Sabbath feeling. Every Sabbath I wonder whether it will happen again; and each time, slowly, a sense of peace comes over me, a sense that everything is as it should be and the world is safe in God's hands.

Afterward, as we walk home, in every house candles flicker. Our house is lit with seven candles, one for each person. In this candle glow, we stand around the table, after the wine is blessed, and we sing.

> *"Thou beautiful Sabbath, thou sanctified day*
> *That chases our cares and sorrows away*
> *Oh come with good fortune, with joy and with peace*
> *To the homes of thy pious, their bliss to increase."*

But poor Meister Jakon, the singer, must spend his Sabbath in the tower, under guard. The next day his wife, pale and trembling, walks from house to house, telling the news, as if by sharing the burden it will weigh less upon her back. "Gone," she says. "He is gone."

"Gone?" Mother pulls her indoors. "What has happened, my dear lady?"

"They said he died under questioning. They questioned him for that old crime—the child who was murdered in Strasbourg. He had nothing to do with it! How could they imagine he had anything to do with it? Meister Jakon loves children."

"Did someone name him? Was there any evidence?"

The wife shakes her head. "What does it matter now? He is gone. They said his heart was bad."

For a moment I watch my mother trying to console the newly made widow. I feel clumsy and helpless. "I'm going," I call, and I hurry to Elias's place to find my friend and perchance to catch a glimpse of Margarite.

Jacob is working in the yard, digging a trench to bury the bones and entrails of slaughtered animals. His face glistens with sweat; his tunic is stained. He looks as strong as any woodsman or hunter. At the window, I glimpse a flash of red hair, then only empty space.

I tell Jacob, "Meister Jakon, the singer, is dead. They said his heart was bad. His wife says he was never ill. Can it be?"

"It's possible," says Jacob, thrusting his foot hard onto the spade. "More likely he was tortured. Gave out."

"But why the singer? That harmless man . . ."

Jacob leans into the shovel, splits the earth with a slicing sound. "He has a fine house," says Jacob. "And a fine garden."

"They will take it?" I know the answer.

"Most certainly. The singer's crime is that he is well off. And proud. You know they don't like to see a Jew walking around with his head high. This town"—Jacob leans on the shovel and glances nervously at the sky—"this town has its darkness."

"They say he was involved in that murder years ago."

"Ah, yes. Murder of a Christian child. And now, after all these years, they point to the singer." Jacob shakes his head. "No. I don't like it. It portends . . ."

Margarite is suddenly there beside us. "Good afternoon, Johannes." Her eyes are downcast, but there is a slight, secret smile about her lips. "Mother says you are to wash up and come to supper," she tells Jacob.

"Directly," says Jacob. He scoops out another large shovelful of soil, tosses it onto the mound as if it were a feather's weight. His arms ripple. The smell of male sweat and strength streams from his body. I feel a terrible clutching at my chest. There is something indecent in Jacob's movements.

Margarite disappears. Jacob pulls yet another load of soil from the reluctant earth. "Lovely young lady, that Margarite," says Jacob. "Well formed." He laughs. "Last week, quite by accident, I happened into the room when she was bathing—"

I am exploding with rage; I leap upon Jacob's back, forcing him down into the dirt, kicking, punching, screaming, "How dare you speak thus of a lady!"

We struggle. Quickly he presses me down flat. I feel the stones in my back. He pins my wrists down over my head. Jacob's face is slick with sweat and blood, streaked with dirt, and he is laughing. "You idiot. I saw nothing. And if I did, her father would have thrashed me, and she herself would have driven me from the house."

"I saw how she looked at you." I lie helpless beneath that looming mass of muscle. "And now you laugh at me."

"Yes, I laugh at you," says Jacob, loosening his hold and dodging one last, swift blow from my fist. "You don't even know that she adores you. I try to talk to her. She only tosses her head. There is only one subject she will discuss, only one name she lingers over."

Slowly I rise, brushing away the stains. I am bruised; my lip is split. It hurts when I smile, and I ask, "Truly?"

"I would not joke about such matters."

"I'm sorry I . . . attacked you."

"No harm. Forget it, brother."

We walk together to the bucket of water. We wash. Jacob, his face and hair dripping, turns to me. "Marry that girl and make it soon. I want to dance at your wedding, but I don't want to stay here forever."

"Don't leave, Jacob! Why would you leave? We have been friends since I was born."

"We will always be friends," says Jacob. "Don't look so sober!"

I do not notice the bucket standing there, until Jacob scoops it up.

"Stop!" I shout. Too late. The water rushes over my head. I am laughing, dripping and cold. Maybe I can find a way to make Jacob stay.

CHAPTER
THIRTEEN

I dream of people spinning round and round in a large room. Their faces are covered with masks. I reach out, wanting to touch someone, but it is forbidden. People speak words without meanings, a constant babble. Bright lights accost me. Sounds hammer into my skin, vibrating, tearing, roaring, sending me flying. "Drome, drome," say the people. "Drome, drome."

All day Grandmother sits in her chair, propped on both sides by pillows. With each breath there is a cluttered wheezing, as if the humors in her chest were struggling to break up and expel themselves. But they remain deep in her bowels, weighing her down. At night she sleeps sitting up, her swollen legs raised onto a low bench. Each breath ends in a moan. I cannot imagine a night of pure rest anymore, for the darkness is punctuated by the sounds of Grandmother's struggle.

Mother is exhausted from tending her. Father is dazed from worry.

Women come. Margarite and her mother brings teas, freshly prepared, steeped until the brew is dark and thick. Frau Freda brings compresses, and she kneads the flesh of Grandmother's swollen legs in her strong hands. The surgeon, Yossi, comes with his blade and his cup to relieve the thick humors that plug Grandmother's veins and bring the swelling to her abdomen and legs. Carefully he cuts, drains, ponders the flow, its color and rhythm.

Grandmother murmurs her thanks and blesses him, but when he is gone she speaks out. "No more," she says with that fierce light in her eyes. "No more healers and bloodlettings and bitter tea. I have done all of it. I have made my peace. Now, let me be."

Grandfather totters around the house in bewilderment. He bumps into the table. He trips on nothing at all. If the children speak to him, he is startled. At supper time he sits with his spoon held over the soup bowl, as if he has quite forgotten what he was doing.

I consult with Jacob. "Her bodily humors are imbalanced," he tells me. "She has always been of moist disposition as I recall. Now moisture collects in her legs and feet. Of course, the moon's cycle also influences these matters."

"Will she die?"

"It is in God's hands," replies Jacob.

I sleep with my ears open. Sometimes I awaken and watch Benjamin on the pallet beside mine, and I hear Grandmother's wheezing and groaning, and I pray in gratitude for each breath that she takes.

One autumn day, I am alone in the house with Grandmother. Grandfather is in the garden digging up stones—for what purpose? Nobody knows. Mother and Rochele are off with their baskets, and Father has gone to return a pledge. Benjamin is working with Rabbi Meier, learning Torah.

I am working out sums on a slate, calculations for our business. I hear the scratch of my stylus between the sounds of Grandmother's rasping breath. But something changes. A brief violence asserts itself—a rumble. I rush to her side.

"Johannes," she rasps. "Johannes!" There is a pale fire in her eyes.

"Let me help you. Some water, perhaps?" I rub her cold hands.

"No." She pulls in air, each breath is like a small storm. She points to the doorway, squinting. "It is very bright. Flying. I'm . . . *flying*!" Her whispers rustle like the dry leaves outside. "Your uncle David. The music you played—the wedding . . ."

My heart swells with longing and pain. "The wedding song."

Grandmother's hand flutters in the air. "Don't you see? We are the bride. Israel. We meet the bridegroom without fear but in love."

"In love," I whisper, feeling the sobs collecting in my chest.

Grandmother touches my face. "This body," she whispers, "is an old garment. Let it lie in a chair. Rejoice. Like the bride and groom. It is this we were made for. This . . . flight."

"I love you, Grandmother!" I call out. I want to enfold her entirely, lend her my breath and my strength, but she is already too distant. There is a gleam in her eye. She sees something.

"Johannes, Johannes," she whispers. "You have the music in you. Make the music. Keep the music."

Her hand drops from my cheek. The moment stretches. I know I should call Grandfather, but something holds me here. I understand now what our sages meant when they said that for the righteous person the moment of death is better than the moment of birth. Grandmother is gone, but something of her is more truly present than ever before.

Two times sitting *shivah* within a single month; it is remarkable. Everyone talks. Ill luck comes in threes. The third comes without warning. A knock at the door.

"Menachem, the moneylender."

"Yes? Yes?"

"You are wanted for questioning."

"What are you talking about? Who wants me?"

"You are to come to the council chambers. The judges will explain. Hurry now, they are waiting, and we don't want to keep them from their work."

"What work? What in God's name? . . . There must be some mistake. Who named me? I have paid my taxes. Ask Herr Swarber. He knows. I always pay—"

"Menachem, what is it?" Mother stands at the door, wringing the linen cloth in her hands. "What do they want?"

"Nothing. It is nothing, Miriam. They want to ask me some questions."

"What questions? Let them come in! Come in, gentlemen. We can talk here."

"It is not how these things are done. You are to come with us to the council chambers. Immediately."

Terror grips me, like iron bands across my chest. I hurry to the door to stand beside my father. I am nearly as tall as he, but I feel larger. I want to pull him away, to bind my arms around him and keep him close. I want to shout at the magistrate, "Leave him alone! Take me. I will answer your foul questions!" But Father throws me a thunderous look that commands silence.

"Look, gentlemen," says Father in his most sonorous voice, "there has been some mistake, I'm sure. I am not the only moneylender here, and my accounts are in perfect order. Let me show you."

"We have nothing to do with accounts. Come now, it is a serious business to keep the judges waiting."

"Well, allow me only to get my ledgers—"

"Nothing is needed. You will be home before dark, I assure you. Such a fuss over a few questions! If a man is innocent, what has he to fear?"

Mother's face is set into stone. She gives me a push. "Go and get Benjamin," she says. "And tell the rabbi."

I go, with Rochele clinging to my hand. "Take me with you, Johannes!" she cries.

Mother nods her consent. She stands at the door like a ghost, pale and motionless, her white skirts fluttering behind her in the sudden wind.

"What are they going to do to Father?" Rochele asks. Her voice is low, not at all the high-pitched voice of a child.

"They said only questions. Surely he will be home before long. Father is smart. He knows what to tell them. He knows how to take care of himself."

The streets are strangely silent. Nobody is about. But a voice accosts us. "You want to know something?"

My stomach tightens. I feel a sharp pull from Rochele and see that she is trembling. "Pay him no mind," I murmur, pulling Rochele along.

Konrad lounges by the church gate. The churchyard is in the shadow of the Jewish quarter, so that at eventide the shadow of the cross falls upon the Jewish streets.

"You! I am speaking to you!" Suddenly Konrad is standing before us, arms folded over his chest. With him is a lanky boy named Rudi. Rudi's head is shorn, with some bristles now growing after the treatment for head lice. His hands are large, the knuckles red and raw looking. He cracks his knuckles, flexes his hands.

"What do you want?" I call out.

"They have your father in the lower chamber," says Konrad. He sways. He moves from one foot to the other, completely at ease, his hands locked behind his back, like a spectator at some play. "I know. I saw them bring him in."

Rochele's legs are shaking. I strain to keep her upright and near.

"You want to know what they do to people in the lower chamber?"

I pull Rochele along beside me as we walk past the two boys. "I'm not interested," I call. We hear the disgusting sound of phlegm being brought up and spat out.

"Wait until you see him," Konrad shouts after us. "You will be interested, I'm sure."

Rude laughter follows us down the street, and a handful of small stones. My heart is beating so madly that I can neither think nor speak.

"I hate him," says Rochele. "The time he caught me and"—she is panting—"you know what he did to me. He tied me up."

"Yes. To a tree."

"And then he . . . he said he was looking for my horns, and he . . ."

"Yes. He is an evil boy."

"I didn't cry, Johannes. I never cried, not once."

"I know. You were brave. Like now. I'm glad you don't cry."

Now we must get Benjamin and tell him. How? We knock at the door of Rabbi Meier's house. The rabbi himself greets us, smiling and nodding. "Your brother, Benjamin, has turned out to be a wonderful scholar!" The rabbi is beaming with pleasure. "We are beginning Talmud. His translations, his questions and comments—but what is the matter, Johannes?"

Swiftly I tell him. The rabbi pulls on his cloak. "I will go down to the council chambers and inquire," he says. He motions to his two sons. "Come with me. Johannes, go home and comfort your dear mother. We will get to the bottom of this, don't worry. And don't forget the evening prayers!"

Benjamin asks the same questions again and again, until it is finally clear to him. Then he walks with his head down, holding his book under his arm. Unwittingly, Rochele kicks up dirt. Benjamin screams out, "Stop it! Stop it!"

"Benjamin." I chide him, nothing more. I can hear the panic in my brother's voice. I see it in the beating vein at his temple. I will divert him. "What did you learn today?"

"Nothing."

"Of course you learned." My tone is stern. "Did you translate your portion?"

"Yes."

"And what was in it?"

"Moses, dying. Because of his sin, he will die upon the mountain. He will not be allowed to cross the Jordan or to lead his people across."

"What was the sin?"

"He did not bless God before the people when he was told to touch the rock and get water from it. He took the credit himself. Johannes, when is Father coming home? What are they doing to him? Where is he?"

"Does Rabbi Meier tell you what we are to learn from this?" I remember all the hours of lessons and translations and then the inevitable question, with the rabbi standing over me, bent to hear my answer to the perennial question: "And what, my child, do we learn from this?" Now I ask Benjamin again.

Benjamin says, "We learn that we must bless God for everything that happens."

"Everything," I repeat. "Whether we think it is good or evil, we bless God, because we do not understand His ways." My own words amaze me. I have never preached to my brother or to anyone. How dare I give lessons to my brother? But then there is nobody else to still the terror in Benjamin's eyes, and someone must do it.

Night comes. Father is still gone. We sit up until the candles are done. Mother stays by our beds with us in the darkness. A trace of moonlight defines her face. "Tomorrow," she says, "if Father is not back, we will go to the council chambers and offer them . . ." She glances toward the money box.

I nod. I will be the one to carry the coins with which to bribe the officials, to beg them to let Father go. "How much will we offer?"

"Everything," says Mother. "Everything we have."

But in the morning, as the cock crows, there is a thumping at the door, and it is Father—or someone who was Father. This man is aged and shrunken. The eyes seem to be pulled backward into their sockets, and the shoulders are hunched. Something is wound around his right arm, a dark cloth; and as he crosses the threshold, he falls.

Mother, Grandfather, and I lift his head, bring him to the bed. He refuses to lie down but sits slumped over. His tongue is thick, his speech oddly slurred. "I told them nothing."

"Menachem, Menachem! Thank God!" Mother kisses his hand, the one that is not bound.

"I told them nothing."

"They released you! Thank God!"

"Peter Swarber. Vouched for me at last, after they—"

"Who did this to you?" asks Grandfather.

"The judges and—for a moment I saw . . . the rings on his fingers. He was by the door, watching."

"Who? Who?"

I speak out. "He means the bishop. Bishop Berthold, may he rot in hell!"

All day we sit beside Father. There is nothing else to do but to pray and to let the flesh mend. Details emerge in small bursts as Father relives the awful night. I had heard about torture, but now I know the reality. The way they twisted his hand. The way they tied the rope and hung him up by the arm and pulled and pulled until the muscles swelled and finally the bones snapped.

Father's voice is weak and rasping. "I told them nothing. What could I confess? Lies? No. I told them the truth. They accused me—"

"Who named you?"

"A man I don't even know. Liebkind, they called him. From Berne. Said the Jews had conspired to kill Christian children."

"That old libel? My God! Why now? Why now?"

"Liebkind says we do it to retaliate for the Jews that were killed by the Armleather gang."

It cannot be told all at once, but in stages.

"Liebkind was tortured. Asked to name names. How did he know my name? Maybe he heard it somewhere. Maybe at the fair. I don't know. But he named me. He also named Meister Jakon; but Jakon died at the very first turn of the rack."

I know how they do it, the methods they use to make people talk. They suggest, then turn the crank, suggest, increase the pain: "It was Meister Jakon, wasn't it? The singer? Yes, it was he, wasn't it? Can we help you remember? Twist another turn, and another. Ah, I think now his memory is improving. And Menachem, wasn't it he? The moneylender? The one with the house and the garden and even a horse? He thinks he is quite the nobleman, coming into people's homes, accosting them for money. It was Menachem, wasn't it, who worked with you to take revenge, wasn't it? Another turn—he is remembering . . ."

Father's arm will be useless forever, also the hand. It changes everything. It changes Father's stance and his gait; it changes the expression on his face. It takes the strength out of his heart and the life out of his eyes. Every morning and afternoon he still stands in prayer, but he bobs and mouths the words. They fall from his mouth like pebbles into a pond. Does he know what he is saying? He and Grandfather, two old men going through the motions of living, leave the efforts of daily life to the younger.

Now, each day, I am the one who goes out to the shops and the estates and the monasteries to try to continue the family business. I decide when to lend and for what sort of pledge. I declare the interest due. I haunt the creditors for repayment.

I, Johannes, the moneylender, look neither to the right nor to the left until late in the day when I reach the house of Elias, the butcher. Then I stand outside, waiting for Margarite to come to the window.

I have brought my flute, and I play to her, songs without words, songs of love.

I know now that life is too short for waiting. I know that Father and Grandfather, immersed in their separate pain, cannot be expected to think about me and my future. But my future cannot be delayed. It belongs to me! I feel a new urgency. I must have Margarite as my wife.

CHAPTER
FOURTEEN

One day after returning home with a goodly commission, I approach my father. It is a fortuitous moment, and I begin without prelude. "Father, I want to marry Margarite."

Father lifts his hand to forestall discussion. "Since when do young people make such decisions for themselves?" he grumbles.

I reply, "Uncle David thought it quite time, Father. I am nearly seventeen, older than you when you and Mother were married."

"Those were different times," he says.

"Times are always different," I reply.

"You take too much upon yourself!" he exclaims. "You have had altogether too much freedom, coming and going—"

"I go only to do the family business, Father."

"It is out of the question now," Father says. "Elias has no money for a bride-price. We would only shame him by asking. We would cause him embarrassment."

"I want no bride-price!" I exclaim. "I only want a bride." How can anyone think of price?

"Have you no pride?" Father retorts. "These things are done according to tradition. Do you think that you can separate yourself from the ages?"

"Father, please," I murmur, only to pacify him, for my blood is racing—and in truth, I have no pride, no thought for anything but Margarite. "Perhaps there is a dowry already put by for Margarite. Perhaps she herself will earn it from her herbs."

"And what of the future?" Father cries. "How do you think you will live?"

"I *am* thinking of the future." My voice rings out sharply. But then, seeing Father's terrible pallor, I lower my voice. I realize now, it is not my future that troubles him but his and Mother's. I draw back and duck my head respectfully. "Father," I say softly, "I will continue to conduct the family business. I will work hard to care for you and Mother in your old age, and for Grandfather. I will do everything, I swear it. I can be both son and husband."

Father looks up, as if he has not really seen me in weeks. His eyes are fixed on my face, my form. "It is true," he finally says. "You are a man. And I have seen how you make valuations and repairs. You know the coinage and the trades." For a moment he places his hand over his eyes. When he looks at me again, I see a faint twitching of his lips.

"So, you are wishing to be married, is it, my son?"

"Yes, Father. Ardently. To Margarite."

"And you think she will have you? And her family will want you for a son-in-law?"

"Not that I am worthy!" I exclaim. "But I have reason to hope— Margarite gave me a talisman when I left for the fair. She speaks with me and she smiles at me."

My father's eyes sparkle now. "I know, my son. Do you think I have not seen how she looks at you?" He rubs his upper lip. "These are delicate matters. I must visit Elias, propose a match, see what can be done about—well, the arrangements."

"Thank you, Father!" I exclaim, and in the next moment my father's arm clasps me tight. I do not think I can remember such a time; my heart overflows with joy.

Margarite's house is decked with flowers and wreaths of pine and spruce and aspen. The days are already touched with the chill of late autumn, but a large wooden table is set outside with tankards of cider and ale, and beautifully decorated loaves of twisted bread, and cakes filled with almond paste, apples, raisins, and spices.

Margarite's mother, Chava, wears a bodice of blue, sleeves of white lace, and a wide, ruffled collar to match. Her skirt rustles as she hurries to and fro greeting guests, receiving congratulations for the betrothal.

Margarite and I stand under the wide-branched willow tree. It drops small green pods around us, like gems from the sky. Beneath our feet is the crunching of autumn leaves, precursor to the glass that I will crush under my foot as a bridegroom at our wedding in the spring.

"I betroth thee to me," I say in a firm, clear voice. My mother is smiling and weeping at the same time. I pass the gold ring with its sapphire stone to Margarite's father. Elias returns it with a nod, then I place the ring on Margarite's finger, feeling the warmth from her hands like a flame. I can imagine how it will feel to hold her in my arms. Everything will be as she wishes it. Everything! She will never know harm or hunger or despair.

Rabbi Meier raises the cup of wine. The knot is tied; God is invoked as witness to the promise. Of course, from now until early spring when the wedding rites are performed, we are still forbidden to each other. But we shall meet and talk and plan.

If I had my way we would be married this very day. But Margarite needs time to prepare herself—to earn money, and to provide linens and candles and clothing for herself—and to make soft blankets for the little ones, God willing. By spring we will decide where to live—whether with my parents or hers, until we can make a home of our own.

Now come the music and the dancing. Moshe with his fiddle leads the way. The young men form a circle. One leaps into the center; the others surround him, all clapping to the beat. "Johannes! Play for us!" they shout.

It is unusual for the celebrant to play at his own feast, but they urge me. I play the dancing tunes and the songs of the seasons, the holiday tunes of thanksgiving. Lastly I play the song of hope that surrounds every occasion whether tragic or festive:

> *I believe in the coming of* Moshiach,
> *And though he may tarry,*
> *Still I await him every day . . .*

It is just past the new year, Yom Kippur, with its fasting and prayer. The synagogue was full, as always. Nobody would stay home during these holy days. People greet each other in the courtyard and on the streets: "May you be inscribed and sealed for a good year! A blessed year of peace and good health and happiness." I feel both more solemn and more buoyant, on the brink of a new life.

The last fruits fall from the trees. The final harvest is in. Margarite and I go one day to the edge of the forest, with Benjamin and the two little sisters along, to gather pinecones and nuts. Benjamin wades into a pond to catch the minnows, and Rochele and Rosa squeal with delight. We see two shapes up on the opposite bank, a boy and a woman, both with fishing rods.

"Hullo," I call, waving. It is Gunther and his mother.

Gunther waves back. "No luck," he calls, pointing to the empty pail, and his mother frowns and nods. *"Grüss Gott!"*

I go to them and tell Gunther, "I am betrothed now, to be wed next spring."

"Congratulations, Johannes," says Gunther, extending his hand. We touch. "Is it the butcher's daughter, then?"

"Indeed." I know I am beaming. "Margarite." I love to say her name.

"A beautiful name," says Greta with a wink. "May you fare well," she continues, "and none of these rumors affect you."

"What rumors?" I ask. Margarite approaches and shyly bids Gunther and Greta, *"Grüss Gott."*

"Why, 'tis nothing to concern us here, I suppose," says Greta with a swift glance at her son. "You know how talk flies from place to place."

"What place?" I inquire.

Greta is biting her lip. "I heard nothing myself," she continues, "but Gunther, who is now with the council—you see his official cap, the one they gave him—he hears things."

Gunther jerks suddenly on his pole, pulls back furiously, and extracts a small fish from the water. It is ridiculous, half the width of his hand. Gunther pries out the hook and tosses it back, wiping his palm on his breeches. "Not much to speak of," he says, "but some Jew was arrested at Lake Geneva. That is in Switzerland."

I hear Margarite's sharp intake of breath. "Switzerland? But that is very far away from us, isn't it? What has it to do with us?"

"Yes—well," says Gunther. "The councilmen are always blabbing on, you know."

"Be respectful of your betters, my son," interrupts his mother.

Gunther looks me in the eye, and I feel a strange chill. "I don't know much about it," he says.

"What happened to the Jew who was arrested?" I do not want to ask, but I must. Whatever one Jew does affects all others.

"I heard he was taken into the castle at Chillon," says Gunther.

"What happened then?" asks Margarite. The little girls come running over. Margarite holds out her hands as if to shield them. Benjamin stands close beside us. "What is it?" he asks fearfully.

"Some Jew was arrested," I tell him.

"What happened to him?" asks Benjamin.

"You know," says Gunther. "The usual."

Greta's mouth is working, her lips twist. "*Ach,* we should not be the ones bringing you this news."

We hear the thud of hoofbeats; horse and rider are decked out richly. The man's cloak is lined with fur, his breeches are velvet. The horse's mane is ornamented, the saddle beautifully tooled. I see the flint-eyed expression on both man and beast.

"Engelbracht," murmurs Greta, hands flying up to her face. "Come, Gunther! We must go."

"One moment!" I call, but they have already turned away, as if to outrun their own shadows.

The little girls fling their sacks full of nuts over their shoulders. Benjamin holds an armful of pine boughs. Margarite and I leave everything there.

"What's the matter?" wails Rosa. "Why are you so glum?"

"Nothing, nothing," says Margarite. But the very air has been altered, as if a sheet of ice has come down over the town. A chill wind whips at our faces and blows through our hair.

"It feels like snow," says Benjamin. "I must go and put Matilda into the shed."

Margarite and I glance at each other. We both burst out laughing. Oh, it is good to be laughing when fear is lapping at your heels! At Margarite's house the door is wide open. People are in the streets, neighbor confronting neighbor. "Have you heard?"

"They say a Jew was arrested."

"So far away, in Switzerland! What has it to do with us?"

"He confessed."

My mother hurries toward us. With her is Frau Freda; behind them comes Rabbi Meier and his two sons. Soon the air rings with the clatter of voices and an air of panic. "His name, they say, is Agimet."

"Agimet?" Soon everyone will know it. Agimet.

"And what do they say this Jew did?" Reb Zebulon, the teacher, steps into the fray, the voice of reason, of composure. "What facts do we have?"

Rabbi Meier's son Ashur steps forward. "I heard it from a traveling notary who came from Zurich, who heard it from an innkeeper." The young scholar takes a deep breath. He is trembling. "This Jew, Agimet, was arrested and taken into the dungeon at the castle. There he was tortured until he confessed."

A hush falls over the people, sudden as snow, still as deepest winter. The word *confessed* strikes everyone alike. Even Zebulon, the teacher, turns pale, and his lips look suddenly swollen as he repeats, "Confessed?"

Now Father has come, and he stands with us, the useless arm tied with a sling across his breast.

Ashur, the son of Rabbi Meier, continues. "The Jew, Agimet, said that he did poison all the wells and that through this poison he brought the pestilence that has killed so many people."

Everyone speaks at once. Vivelin Rote, the wealthiest among us, knocks his walking stick on the ground. "Where is this informant? The notary? We want to question him."

"Quickly go," Rabbi Meier tells his son, "fetch him to us. We must hear everything. Come!" He motions to the congregation. "We'll go to the synagogue for meeting. Let us not gather like cattle on the street, letting our distress spill out for all our enemies to satiate their lust."

Now I see that numbers of gentiles have come around. They listen and lurch to and fro, prodding one another with pointed fingers: *See? See? They are all in conspiracy against us.* And from a tree, looking down, a rude voice calls, "You want to know something?"

The elders have already moved toward the synagogue, a rushing, pulsating throng, eager to get indoors. But Benjamin and Jacob and I hang back, and I see the face of that hateful snake with the hair like straw, and the other boy, lanky and lean and scowling.

"We want to know nothing from you!" I shout. I have had enough, and more than enough.

"Come away, Johannes," Jacob pleads.

But Konrad and Rudi swing down from the large limbs, land with a thud and crackle of tree bark and dry leaves. Konrad takes a stance, fists braced on his hips, and Rudi follows him.

"You want to know something? My father told us this Jew bled from every orifice when they tortured him," says Konrad. "He confessed, finally. He said he brought the poison in a small red pouch and put it into the wells to kill all the Christians. But now they've caught him, and they'll make him pay, and we are going to get all the rest of you, my father said so!"

"Stinking ass!" shouts Jacob, the veins throbbing at his throat. "What nonsense you speak. Don't you know that Jews are also dying of the pestilence?"

"It's a trick," shouts Konrad. "They take a few of their own to make themselves look innocent. We know the truth. My father says—"

"May your father rot in purgatory!" screams Benjamin.

The race is on, we three Jews flying along the street, Konrad and Rudi darting after us, throwing sticks and stones. But this time we are faster. Benjamin, in the lead, scrambles away, scales a wall, leaps down. Jacob and I follow. I feel something flying past my head—a stick, then another. But inside I feel no rage, only this power. We have bested Konard and we are safe!

Inside the synagogue, a small sanctuary, the community is crowded together around the lectern. Candles are lit, as dusk is fast approaching. People whisper and shuffle; it seems wrong to make noise.

Ashur, son of Rabbi Meier, appears at last with the notary in tow. The notary is a thin man with a half-moon face, long of chin and beard. His brows jerk up at every new sentence, but he speaks smoothly and clearly, while the people gather round, men and women and children hanging on his words.

"Well, it has been said all over that this pestilence and all the deaths must be due to some conspiracy. So they said it must be the Jews, for they desire to kill the Christians. Someone said that some Jews in Toledo initiated the plot, that one of the chief conspirators was a rabbi named Peyret, who had his headquarters in Savoy and dispatched various poisoners to Italy and Switzerland and France."

Shadows seem to snap along the walls, rising and shrinking with the candle flames. And it is cold, cold as death in this sanctuary.

Reb Zebulon, impatient, prods the speaker. "What next, man? Don't keep us waiting!"

The notary licks his lips, then swallows. "Well, so Lord Amadeus, the Count of Savoy, ordered the arrest of a number of the Jews who lived on the shores of Lake Geneva. They were brought to the castle. There they were tortured. You know how those inquisitions go." The man's eyes dart around the room, seeking a focus, and finding none, drop down to the floor. "They had Agimet for many hours. At last he confessed."

"Confessed to what, exactly?" cries the rabbi, his face bloated in the candle glow, hands outspread.

"Said this rabbi named Peyret had sent for him; for he, Agimet, was a silk merchant and known to travel afar. So the rabbi thought to use him for this plot and gave him a little package, half a span in size, which contained some prepared poison in a thin sewed leather bag. And he said to distribute it along the wells, cisterns, and springs about Venice and the other places to which he would go, in order to poison the people who use the wells for drinking."

Not one voice is raised now, not one sound is heard. It is too preposterous a lie, too strange and complicated. And yet, the lie will live. We all know it. The name Agimet will be bound up with this lie forever.

The man continues, dropping his words into the cold gray shadows, into our minds, as we stand awestruck and dumbfounded. "So Agimet says he took this package full of poison and carried it to Venice, and when he came there, he threw and scattered it into every well and cistern. He also said that this Rabbi Peyret promised to give him whatever he wanted in return for his troubles in this business. And then Agimet confessed further that he went and put poison into the wells near the Mediterranean Sea and everywhere. They asked if any of the Jews in those places were also guilty, and he said he did not know. But he swore on the five books of Moses."

My father speaks. "Poor wretch. They broke him."

Nobody answers. All understand that only by the grace of God and the intercession of Councilman Peter Swarber, Menachem did not break. How long could anyone hold out? The people suck in air. They drag and scuffle their feet. Everyone wants to go home.

The rabbi opens the doors and all depart. I have lost sight of Margarite. And, in truth, I do not want to see her now, for I can offer her no comfort. At home we sit in the dark and finally go to our beds.

Softly into the darkness Benjamin whispers, "Do they think we are in on it, too?"

I pretend to be asleep. I know that the gentiles think all Jews are connected and all are one, the same. Whatever happens to Agimet could happen to us, too.

N ow every morning four of us stand together in prayer, for Benjamin, following his bar mitzvah, is also putting on his prayer shawl and tefillin. We stand by the door, where the morning light greets us. We say, "May He remember that He promised us the coming of *Moshiach*—may he come in our lifetime . . ."

Now that I am betrothed to Margarite, sometimes I feel almost as if *Moshiach* has already come. There is a gladness in me that I never knew before.

We speak every day of *Moshiach*, not because life is so bad on Earth, for has not God provided all we need? What we seek from *Moshiach* is order and holiness and love. We pray that soon, very soon, a great leader will emerge from among the people, to bring us to sanity and love. And it is this idea that puts the knife blade between Jew and gentile—the question of whether he has already come, and whether he is man or God.

Yes, I pray daily for the coming of *Moshiach*, but in truth, what I really await is springtime and Margarite. I am content in my anticipation.

But news encroaches, arriving slowly at first, then raging like floodwater. Within hours everybody knows what Herr Fritsche Closener learned from his correspondents, what Baron Zorn boasted about in the tavern, what Count Engelbracht told to his companions on the hunt: Some Christians are murdering Jews, accusing them of bringing the pestilence. Pope Clement VI defends the Jews, issuing an edict from his palace in Avignon. "Christians who imagine that the Jews are responsible for this pestilence have been seduced by that liar the devil!"

No stronger words have ever been issued by a ruling pope, including the admonition that Jews are not to be robbed or forcibly converted or killed without a proper trial. But local clergy do not listen to the pope—they have their own opinions and their own reasons. After the confession of Agimet, many Jews in various towns were killed by mobs. Some voices were raised in outrage: What about the city council? The police? Well, these were the random acts of a few thugs—never mind. Why do the Jews always feel so persecuted? Why can't they be calm?

Soon we hear that the city council of Zurich has voted to expel the Jews. They are ordered never to return.

"It is like the old days," mourns Grandfather. "When we were expelled from France. What can we do?" He throws up his hands, goes out into the garden, where the winter wind whips branches into his face. He looks for stones.

I am troubled, and I ask my father, "Where will these people go? How can they live? Must they leave their homes and everything behind?"

My father shrugs. "We Jews are accustomed to wandering. They will move to some other place. Maybe to a smaller town, or a larger one. Who knows?"

"Maybe we should leave Strasbourg," I say heavily, though I am torn at the thought of really leaving these streets, this dear house, our friends. "Jacob speaks of a deep darkness in Strasbourg."

Father turns on me with a sudden fury. "Where would we go? Tell me that, my learned son. To France, where they already threw out the Jews? To Italy, which this pestilence laid waste? To Switzerland, where so-called poisoners are seized and tortured and finally cut to pieces?"

My heart hammers with pain and helplessness. "I don't know! I don't know! But they are killing us . . ."

"That is the point, my son," Father says, his face red from shouting. "Where, indeed? Even if we could find our way to the Holy Land, what do you think is left of it, after the crusaders plundered and killed, and destroyed the city? Jerusalem! It lies in ruins." My father paces round and round, his useless right arm hanging limp at his side. "I hear it from the travelers, even the monks. You think I haven't thought about it? Escape? I thought about Spain. They say, now, the whole plot began in Spain. No. Not Spain. The Netherlands? There, too, the Jews must wear the badge. No, not the Netherlands. Maybe to China? Do you think we could find our way to China, my son? And if we did, would we finally have peace?"

Mother suddenly shouts, "Leave the boy alone, Menachem! Leave him alone!"

"He has to learn not to ask ridiculous questions!" Father shouts back.

"He is young. Let him have hope!" she cries.

I stand between the two, distraught. "I'm sorry," I exclaim. "Let it be. Please don't quarrel over my stupidity."

Father's head is thrown back, eyes shut in pain. "Oh God, it is not stupidity," he says. "It is fear and worry and the need to take action—all these I have also felt, my son. The truth is, I do not know what to do. I do not know."

Things grow more difficult. One of the prefects of the Franciscan monastery comes to us, needing a loan to repair the roof of his building. He brings as a pledge a beautiful chalice, but he is reluctant to part with the church treasure. He speaks plainly. "How can I entrust this valuable property to a Jew? How do I even know you will be here six months from now, when repayment is due?"

"We will be here," says Father.

"Who will stand in for you?" persists the monk. "Do you know someone who will vouch for you?"

I hold my breath. Two or three gentile citizens, upright church-going tradesmen, used to perform this service for us. They are no longer available, they told us.

"Perhaps," I suggest, "Herr Closener will stand in for us."

Father's brows lift in surprise. "You think you could call upon him?"

"He has invited me to play music with him, Father. He praised us as good messengers to his friend in Troyes."

"Well, if you think it wise, my son." Father steps back, his manner mild; and I feel as if my father and I have changed places.

"I will see to it," I tell the Franciscan. "Please return tomorrow afternoon, and I will have arranged it."

With full confidence, I set out, my flute in my pocket, walking briskly. I go alone, for the winter chill aggravates Father's bad arm. I see an ice blue sky with streaks of white; I hear the scurrying of a few late squirrels, the call of a bird high up on a limb. Bells ring out from St. Thomas—the midafternoon bells. The cobblestones seem tinted with blue and lavender; the pointed rooftops gleam like polished brass. A horse stamps and whinnies, waiting for its master; and I think of Benjamin and that horse, Matilda, its belly now respectably rounded, forelocks shining, and hooves blackened with gleaming pitch. And I cannot understand it. In the midst of this beauty, why is there such trouble in the world?

At the home of Fritsche Closener, I wait at the door, hearing voices from inside. I stand for a time, unwilling to intrude; and just as I turn away, the door is flung open. It is Closener himself, followed by a gentleman with a full white beard and black cloak and, of all things, spectacles before his eyes. I have never seen the like before. The gentleman gazes at me through the lenses, and it is like a double stare, confounded and horrified.

Herr Closener, preceding his guest, does not see the look. "My young friend!" he calls, taking my arm. "Come in, come in. Have you brought us some music? Symont, do stay a few minutes longer, and we shall play for you."

"No, no," says the other, "it is out of the question." He swings his walking stick vigorously. "Quite out of the question, Fritsche. I am wanted back home. Yes, I have heard the bells and I must certainly be on my way." The man coughs. He whirls around to look Closener in the eye, seems about to say more, but turns swiftly and strides away.

"Well," says Herr Closener, "he is a busy man. But come. Surely we have time for a tune or two. Something from the theater at Troyes? Yes?"

My fingers feel tight and stiff, a lingering frost from the cold stare that man Symont turned on me. The music is spoiled, I fear. But then Herr Closener takes up his recorder and stands in readiness; and in spite of myself, I forget the man and the cold and everything but the music.

I play and play, my heart swelling to the remembrance of that melody, the tune that David and I heard when the night was bright with stars. I play the laughter we heard, the whispers, the breeze, the clopping of horses, the rattling of carts, the calling out of merchants, one to the other—ah, will I ever see another fair like that one?

Herr Fritsche Closener listens with his head cocked. He keeps the beat with his hand. Then he lifts the recorder to his lips and matches note for note, bringing in a new trill, a digression, a harmony. We play it again and again—each time different, each time better—and at last we put down our instruments and stand, beaming, our eyes locked upon each other.

Herr Closener is exuberant. "Wonderful! That was great fun. Thank you for bringing it to me. I shall play it again tonight, so as not to forget it; but I think I've got it now." And he plays a few more phrases all alone, nodding his head; then he smiles. "Yes, I've got it, my young friend."

His words "young friend" give me courage to ask the favor: Would Herr Closener so kindly give consent to be present when the prefect from the monastery brings his pledge for money loaned? And might Herr Closener hold the pledge in his keeping, for surety, so that the bargain can be made and the monk not fear for his property?

Herr Closener turns toward his hearth, shaking his head. "Alas, I cannot do this," he says gruffly. "I cannot take sides in this matter. Do you understand? It is one thing to make music. We musicians speak a special language. But to put myself between the church and the . . . the moneylender, no. It would not be right. You see, I am a scribe. I keep records of events. I cannot be in the middle and still see clearly. People must not say that I am—ah—influenced. You understand."

"I understand," I say dully. "You mean the poisoning. You mean the confession."

"Confessions," he corrects me. "More than one. Surely, you have heard?"

"We heard about that man from Chillon, Agimet." I go toward the door feeling desperate, suddenly, to go home, to *be* home, away from this alien place that only a few moments ago felt warm and friendly.

"Ten more Jews were questioned," says Closener. "They confessed that they were all in on the same plot. That, in fact, *all* the Jews, from the age of seven, have known about the plot and participated in it."

My face is hot, as if I were standing by the fire, although I am really half out the door. "They were tortured," I say. "Like my father."

"Yes, of course they were!" cries Closener. He takes a leap toward me, rakes his hands through his hair, straining. "I know that, and we all know it. They would confess to anything after being put on the rack—who wouldn't? But the confessions are being spread swiftly abroad, and they accuse every Jew. *Every* Jew from childhood on, as a conspirator, a poisoner of wells, a bringer of pestilence."

"So they accuse." I feel light-headed, faint. I steady myself on the door frame.

"They accuse and they burn."

"Burn?"

"In Basel." Closener looks down, shakes his head. "They shut up all the Jews in a large wooden house. Set it on fire."

"They burned the Jews?"

"They did burn the Jews."

As I leave I hear Closener muttering, "Money was indeed the thing that killed the Jews. If they had been poor, and if the feudal lords had not been in debt to them, they would not have been burned."

His words keep changing into images in my mind, questions and answers piling up like dead wood all around me, until I feel

closed in and suffocated. *They built a large wooden house* . . . I see it
in my mind's eye, the large wooden structure built in a field, and
a door through which the Jews enter, which can then be nailed
shut. The roof is flimsy, no more than a few simple boards thrown
over the walls, with spaces wide enough for the flames to leap
through. And inside . . . inside . . . inside the people are pressed
tightly together—arms, shoulders, legs, and heads all touching.
Women cradle their babies in their arms. Fathers and mothers
hold young children tight. They murmur reassurance: *It's all right,
really, don't cry. Don't be afraid.*

How do they light the structure? With torches, many at once, so
that the blaze seems to jump from spot to spot, and the structure
fills with smoke, the more because the wood is green. But the
cheering crowd likes it that way, for the smoke is thick and dark,
rising skyward, a signal and a sign of what happens to heretics.
The flames, popping and sizzling, create their own symphony,
matching the cries from within. How long does it take, this burning? Inside, does it seem like forever? Or are their minds and bodies frozen, so that it seems but a flash, a swift flight to oblivion?

Usually I do not pray apart from the set times. Now I pray over
and over, "Master of the universe . . . Master of the universe . . .
Help me to understand Thy ways."

Somehow an answer is borne on the wind as it whips thin flakes
of snow across the road: "These are not My ways, but those of men."

I whisper the one prayer that a Jew never forgets. "*Shema Yisroel*
. . . Hear, oh Israel, the Lord our God, the Lord is one." One. Sin-
gular. Indescribable. Unequaled. Unique. We insist that He is one.
For that, they burn us.

I turn down the street where Margarite lives. It is nearly dusk,
and my mother will be wondering about me, but I cannot bear to
go home. I knock. Margarite answers. Her face is flushed from bending over the fire. Her hair is tied back with a white cord, but a few
small curls escape to frame her face, and a long lock clings to her
neck. I feel overcome with desire at the sight of those damp curls. I
would hold her in my arms, but temptation must be abandoned.
Besides, her mother is in the room.

I nod. "Good day, Margarite." I inquire politely, "How is your family? Is Jacob here with you?"

"No," Margarite says. "He is staying with Dr. Yunge. My father cannot keep him here anymore. There is not enough work. But come in, come in, Johannes."

I enter, saying, "It was not Jacob whom I came to see." I am rewarded by Margarite's smile.

"Good evening, Johannes," calls Margarite's mother, Chava. "We all hope you will stay for supper, poor as it is." She is friendly as ever, but something in her face is altered, reluctant.

"Thank you kindly, but I must be home soon. Mama still worries about me when the light dims." I chuckle.

"Of course," says Chava. "Mothers never stop worrying, even when their children are grown. At least have a dish of blackberries. We picked them this afternoon, the last of them, I think."

Margarite brings me a dish of berries, large and ripe, bursting with juice. I murmur the blessing and pop one into my mouth, seeing that Margarite's lips, too, are stained from berry juice. "Delicious!" I say.

Rosa is pale and very quiet today. She glances around. "Isn't Rochele with you? I want to see Rochele."

Her mother smiles slightly. "You saw your friend just yesterday. Come, Rosa, I need you to help me with the mending. Come, come," she says, pulling the little girl to the end of the room, where several chairs and a spinning wheel and small table make a separate space, so that Margarite and I are left with some privacy.

Margarite speaks softly. "My father would greet you," she says, "but he is with the rabbi and some other men, deep in discussion. It is terrible for him. Today . . . it is terrible for him," she repeats.

"What is it?" I ask. "The confessions?"

"What confessions?"

"Some Jews confessed to poisoning wells everywhere in Europe," I tell her. The burden seems now to have shifted. My main concern is for Margarite, to clear away the trouble in her eyes. I will not tell her about the burning.

"I did not know about any more confessions," she says.

"Then what is it?"

Margarite looks away. "This afternoon," she says, "I was with Father at the mill. Mother and Rosa were picking berries. As we returned home, we heard a terrible outcry. Someone had put a sow into our yard. They had covered it with oil and set it ablaze."

My head throbs. My vision seems altered, blurred. "Who could do such a thing?"

"It was horrible, Johannes, the screams of the pig, and the smoke and the smell . . . You cannot imagine."

"I can imagine."

"Papa ran and put the poor creature out of its misery. There was pig blood all over the yard, all over Papa's hands and arms and apron." Margarite begins to tremble, and she clasps her arms around herself; but she lifts her chin and there is defiance in her eyes, and in her voice. "I told Papa to give them nothing! They are criminals. Rogues. Now Papa and the rabbi and some other men are talking—"

"What do they want from your father? Who is behind this?"

"Look about you, Johannes," Margarite cries with sudden vehemence. "The townspeople are changing toward us. I see it in their faces when I walk through the town. I feel how they despise me."

"No, no, they fear the pestilence, though it has not approached here at all."

Margarite looks down, frowning. "My father had visitors today, after the incident with the pig. Out in the yard. Four men came."

"Who?"

"One was Uriah, the tanner—the one with the arms as big as trees. Two were from the guild association, and then there was that butcher. Betscholt."

"Betscholt," I repeat. "I know him well. And his son."

Margarite continues, her eyes blazing with fury. "They told my father that if he continues to sell meat to gentiles, they will burn our house down. They called him names; and they said the pig is only an example of what will happen to him."

We hear the heavy tread; Elias walks in. He bids me good evening. "Is your family well?" he inquires.

"Yes, thank you. All are well and send you greetings," I reply, sounding calm, though I am sorely shaken.

Elias goes to his wife. "I must pay a heavy fine," he says, "for selling meat to gentiles. And they have imposed an extra tax. They call it a meat tax. If I don't pay it, Chava, I won't have any business at all."

"More taxes!" Chava cries.

"I suppose I must give the extra meat away. Or burn it."

"That's a sacrilege!" Chava exclaims.

"Wife, hear me. If I want to stay in business, I must bribe the guilds. They call it protection from foreign enemies, tax for the use of public roads and waterways. They said I earn my living here, and I must give back something to the guildsmen who make this town prosper. And also to the bishop, who grants protection and privilege."

"Ah, now it is clear," I say. "Bishop Berthold." I am astonished at my rudeness, to join a conversation to which I was not invited. But Elias turns and nods, including me.

"Bishop Berthold reminds us continually that it is he who keeps the Armleather gang from going on a rampage against us. And now," Elias says, his shoulders hunched, "he has still more ammunition. They say that ten Jews have confessed to poisonings. They say it is a conspiracy of all Jews everywhere, desiring to kill all Christians."

I see Margarite's alarm in her frozen stance. Chava gasps and lets the mending fall from her fingers.

"In Basel," says Elias, "they have burned the Jews. They were given the choice to accept Christ . . ." Elias puts out his arms, as if in supplication. He gazes at Rosa, whose eyes are round and wide, and he gathers her in his arms. "Enough," he says. "It is supper time. Johannes, will you stay?"

"No, no, you are most kind, but I must hurry home now."

"Go, then, quickly," says Chava, "before darkness overtakes you."

But darkness has already overtaken me, a terrible darkness that no candle can dispel. I feel sickened and powerless, like the day I saw that infant drowning.

Margarite walks with me to the door. She steps outside. "Johannes, what is happening? Father always said we are safe with the bishop on our side, and the council letting us work and live here. There is no plague in Strasbourg, nor anyplace near."

"It makes no sense," I say. "How can anyone believe it? If we poisoned the water, we would be poisoning ourselves, too."

Margarite stands silently beside me. It is cold, but she does not shiver. "Those people in Basel," she says, "are heroes. They are like Hanna with her seven sons. They are like Rabbi Akiba. I have always wondered whether Hanna was a real person."

"They were all real," I tell her. "Martyrs." I am thinking also of David.

For an instant in the dim light—so brief an instant that it might have been a dream—I feel Margarite's fingertips on my cheek and her lips upon mine.

CHAPTER SIXTEEN

It is rare, these days, for a non-Jew to be seen walking these streets, so I am surprised to see Gunther peering into doorways and alleys, like a cat searching for mice.

"Gunther!" I call out from the window.

Gunther glances about, then hurries over, panting. "I've been looking for you, Johannes. I did not know which house . . . Forgive me, but my mother asked me to find your friend, Dr. Jacob."

"Come inside, Gunther."

"No. I cannot. Is the young doctor there with you?"

A blast of wind makes me shiver. "Wait. I will get my cloak." Outside, I stand opposite Gunther. "Is your mother ill?"

"No. Father. He is red with rash and moaning . . ."

"What could it be?" My heart seems to stop dead still. *What could it be?* Everyone knows that pestilence is the rage and the terror of all Europe! Oh, God, if the pestilence has come to Strasbourg, I do not know what to fear more, the disease or our neighbors—for they will surely say we have brought them this plague. If Gunther's father has the sickness, then perhaps it is borne even on Gunther's clothing, in his breath, his touch—I am afraid to be near him or even to look at him. I have heard that a glance from someone stricken spreads the disease. I stand, immobile, and Gunther is fairly doubled over from distress.

"Jacob is staying with Dr. Yunge," I finally say, breathing hard. "We will go get them." I call to my mother that I am going out, and we hurry along the streets. The edges of the road are banked with snow, and few people are about, save the wood carriers and tinkers and millers with their sacks of grain. The tradespeople nod and give greeting, casting a suspicious, anxious eye upon Gunther.

"Your people don't want me here," Gunther says, panting.

"No, no, it is all right," I say. "They just aren't used to seeing you. But you are with me. Don't worry." I feel Gunther's tension. "Why does your mother send especially for Jacob?"

Gunther bites his lip. "The doctor in town won't come for the likes of us. Mother thought that the Jew doctor, the young one, might come to examine Father, perhaps only to tell us what ails him. Mother cannot pay him, except—do you suppose he would take a cheese?"

"Perhaps." I have not the heart to tell Gunther that Jewish doctors do not eat cheese made with rennet from a nonkosher animal.

We walk on to the house of Dr. Yunge, where Jacob is alone, washing out bottles and filling vials with strange-colored concoctions.

"Dr. Yunge is not here," Jacob says. He glances at us suspiciously. "Is this a visit?"

"Gunther's father needs you," I say. "He has a rash. He moans."

Our eyes meet for a long moment. Jacob takes up a small leather bag, fills it with vials and powders and several pieces of white-and-red cloth. He pulls his cloak down from a nail; it is black wool, worn and pocked with holes. "Come," he says.

We three trudge along the road behind the cathedral, up over the bridge, and to the bottomland, where the small hut sticks out from a deep cushion of snow all around. No smoke comes from the tilting chimney, no sign of warmth or life, until, as we draw nearer, the small windows emit sounds like those of an animal, snarling and snorting, bellowing and shouting. "You damnable sow! You miserable old hag, what do I have to do to get you to bring me something against this pain? If ever you are ill, I swear . . . I can't wait to see you suffer, to pay you back thrust for thrust."

Jacob strides forward and bangs on the door. "Doctor here!" he calls in a new tone, full of stern authority.

The door is pulled open. Inside, the air is dank and putrid. I hold my breath and blink against the darkness and the fumes. At last my eyes become accustomed to the murky interior, and I see a small hearth, a pallet of straw, a table, two chairs, and a stool.

Greta rushes toward us. "Oh, you've come! Bless you, bless you, I knew you would do it, Johannes. Wait, let me light a candle." She hurries to the end of the room and rushes back with a small stub of a candle on a broken dish. The candle flares, illuminating the patient—a dark, heavily bearded hulk of a man. His chest is sunken, but he has powerful arms. His legs are outstretched, lacking feet.

"What is this you have brought me, woman?" he shouts, face contorted with rage and pain. "Mere boys for this affliction? Are you crazy?"

Jacob lifts his hand, taking charge. He moves nearer to the patient, kneeling down, making his voice pleasant, almost light. "Well, what have we here, sir," he says. "A bit of a rash, I hear. And are you able to eat and to expel?"

"Pain," the man roars. He opens his mouth. I smell the stench of rot. His jaw is swollen, also his left cheek.

"Ah, a bad tooth, is it? Much inflamed. Bring the candle closer, if you please."

Greta brings the candle, holds it steady a few centimeters from the husband's gaping dark mouth.

"Put out your tongue, please," says Jacob. I watch in awe as Jacob studies the patient—his mouth, eyes, hair. Jacob touches the man's forehead, peers at the red rash around the mouth and nose and hands. Even from this distance, I can see the red, scaly skin, and the lice that squirm in the man's scalp.

Greta holds the candle up; it flickers, the flame rises. "What is it, Doctor?" she asks, her voice trembling.

"Skin rash," says Jacob, "could be from typhus. But there is no fever, and no diarrhea, I suppose."

"No," bellows the patient, "and a good thing, too, because on these stumps I'd never make it to the hole!"

Now I see a filthy cushion on the floor beside the man. With the cushion under his belly, he must drag himself from place to place. My stomach rises to my mouth. I turn away, wishing for a moment of oblivion until this sickness passes. But I look straight into Gunther's face.

"What shall we do, Doctor?" asks Greta, half bowing.

"The tooth must come out," says Jacob. "I have never done this myself, but—"

"Please," urges Greta. "Do it for him. We have nobody. None of them will see to the likes of us, the barber or the surgeon—"

"Shut your mouth, woman!" bellows the husband, swinging his fists and flailing his footless legs. "If the Jew doesn't want to do it, let him go to hell!"

"I'll do it," says Jacob. He pokes into his bag. In it is a small hammer and a pair of pointed pliers, long armed and powerful. He turns to me and Gunther. "It would be better if you will hold his arms."

Greta draws back.

"No, mistress! We need the light. Be brave," says Jacob. He is glorious, strong, and courageous. I, myself, would never attempt such a feat as to reach inside the smoldering mouth of this madman.

All is still. I squat down and grasp one of the man's arms. It is thick and muscular and hot, despite the icy chill in the cabin. My fingers grow numb, and also my toes. The patient's raw stumps are bound with dark rags, torn and shredded. I curl my toes inside my boots, grateful for my wholeness.

A pull, a grunt, a scream, and it is done. I almost fall back with fright at the howl. A bloody, jagged tooth falls into the basin with a clatter. The patient is limp and silent. Tears streak down his face.

"Now, now," says Jacob, wiping his hands on a cloth, tossing everything back into the bag. "Drink some water later. Don't try to eat. As for the rash"—he turns to Greta—"try to cover this straw pallet with some cloth if you can. I will leave you this special compound of nettle and rose water. You must wash his face and hands with it twice a day, once at prime and again at vespers. He will be fine, God willing."

Greta stands there, wringing her hands, her face creased. "Oh, Doctor, how can I thank you? It is not, it is not . . ." She cannot make herself say the dreaded word.

"No," Jacob says lightly. "It is not the pestilence. Not at all. Only the inflammation from that rotten tooth. Water several times a day. Flush it out. Good luck," he says, motioning to me that we are leaving.

Greta comes out with us. We stand in the bitter cold. I clap my hands together. From inside comes a bellow; the man has revived. "Greta, you old pig, will you desert me now, leave me rotting here?"

Greta nods and winks slowly, moving her lips into a grimace, almost a smile. "It is only since he lost his feet," she says, "that he has been so . . . so hard. He cannot move, you see, except on his belly like a reptile, and then, not very well. So he sits there and hates me, because he needs me. I know I am not to blame. Did I cut off his feet? But he cannot walk, and he cannot take revenge on the soldiers who did it. So he curses me and snarls like a wild beast. I am sorry he is so—well, I thank you. He is, after all, my husband."

She rushes to the small shed, the storehouse for her wares, returning with a round cheese wrapped in cloth. "I have no money," she says, handing the cheese to Jacob.

Jacob quickly puts out his hand and takes the cheese. He smiles. "Thank you, Frau Greta. It smells delicious. Quite delicious."

"We are grateful to you, Herr Dr. Jacob," she says. I see the lift in Jacob's shoulders.

"Not to mention it," says Jacob.

When we are some distance from Greta's house, I say, "They did it so he could not fight again."

"Yes," says Jacob.

"What battle?" I have not concerned myself with such things. Jews are never soldiers; we are forbidden to carry arms.

Jacob says, "Lord Engelbracht staged a raid to the border. He claimed that Count Rheinhold's people were stealing his livestock. Engelbracht's men were routed. Several were killed. The others were maimed so they could not fight again."

"How do you know this?"

Jacob chuckles. "I ask questions. Also, I have traveled a bit."

"What will you do with the cheese?"

"Give it to a gentile, I suppose. Do you know someone?"

"Herr Closener."

"We will take it now," says Jacob, holding the cheese aloft.

We go to Closener's house, three streets east of the cathedral. From Closener's chimney a full column of smoke rises, and from within, the brightness of several lanterns beckons.

In a moment Fritsche Closener answers my knock, appearing with the hound at his heels. Closener looks from right to left, then draws me quickly inside. "Come in, my young friend! Come in!"

"This is my good friend, Jacob, the doctor," I say, stepping inside toward the warmth from the fire.

"Jacob," muses Herr Closener, rubbing his chin. "I know you— ah, yes! I have not seen you since you were a lad. You are a doctor now? How time flies."

Jacob smiles and nods. "I studied in Paris for some years."

"And do you practice here now?"

"I assist Dr. Yunge, but not officially," Jacob says hastily. One never knows what will be repeated.

"To what do I owe the honor of this visit?" asks Closener. "A song or two, perhaps?"

"We have brought you this cheese," says Jacob.

"Ah," says Closener, taking it. "It smells delicious. I suppose it is forbidden to you," he says, eyes bright with curiosity.

"That is true," I say.

"So, it is lucky for me," says Closener with a smile. "Thank you. I will have this wonderful treat with my bread for supper." He pauses, then suddenly bursts out, "I would never ask a man why he does this or that, believes this or that. Belief cannot be reasoned or forced, can it?" Herr Closener's face is flushed, his movements quick and agitated.

"There are those who think otherwise," Jacob says soberly.

"We are fortunate in Strasbourg," says Closener, "with the likes of Peter Swarber and Gosse Sturm on the council. If the hotheads among us had their way—" He stops as the Angelus rings. Soon it will be dark. Jacob and I move toward the door.

"Come again soon," says Closener. "We will make music. I have heard some of your Sabbath songs—lovely, lovely indeed." He walks to the door, then turns back, plucking at his collar nervously. "Look, if I were you," he says, "I would consider . . ." He faces us fully. "I would leave. I would find another place to live."

"Leave?" I echo. "Where would we go?"

"Perhaps to a larger city. Perhaps to the mountains. I don't know." The hound nudges Closener's knee, whimpering. "All right, Wechsel, hush." Closener continues. "Perhaps in Frankfurt, people are . . ." He grimaces. "I don't know. Zurich has expelled its Jews. The rabble are starting up in the German towns and villages, inflamed by the flagellants. You know how it is. Like a mania, it is catching. Maybe in Frankfurt there is less . . . less insanity. I know a doctor there. Perhaps you could go to him. His name is Spitz. Perhaps he could use an assistant."

Jacob's face is flushed and his eyes glow with excitement. "I would go," he says eagerly, "I would go in a moment if the roads were not so terrible. The snow is deep. Perhaps in spring."

"Spring," murmurs Herr Closener. He pats the hound gently. "Well, we hope for the best, don't we? Thank you for stopping. Thank you for the cheese. *Grüss Gott.*"

That night I dream of Margarite, but it is a terrifying dream, for her face is frozen into a mask of blue ice. Her eyes peer out of the mask like black pebbles, and her hair has turned pale as straw. I go to her and try to remove the mask, but my fingers are caught as if in thorns and brambles, and I hear someone screaming, "You will be punished! You will burn!"

When I awaken, each breath brings a sharp pain to my chest. My fingers feel numb. Outside the air is thick with white fog. I can hear the wheels of a lone cart crackling over the ice. I must see Margarite. That ice blue mask, those granite-dead eyes. Perhaps Closener is right. Perhaps we can leave. I will find a cart or a sled, and I will bundle Margarite up beside me to keep her warm and safe.

For a week or more I am too ill to go outdoors. With every breath my chest feels as if a blade is lodged there. Margarite comes and brings chamomile. She brings camphor leaves to brew into a poultice for my chest. She brings a lemon, and this time, too, she has brought Rosa over to play with Rochele while we visit.

"Where on earth did you find a lemon?" I exclaim, rising from the chair. I am feeling better today. Margarite is wearing a soft brown cloak and black boots. A fine haze of snowflakes lies on her hood, like a crown.

She laughs. " 'Tis a secret."

"Tell me!"

She smiles. "Well, Mother had it since the fall. She was saving it for Hanukkah; but it is better that you have it now. You can save the rind for us; we will boil it in sugar to season our Hanukkah cakes. Also I have made you some cookies," she says, "with anise in them for your health."

"I thank you," I say. And then, slowly ask, "You know my gentile friend Fritsche Closener? The one who is a scribe and who plays the recorder?"

"Yes. You have some fine friends, I know it. He is a gentleman and a scholar."

"Herr Closener thinks that . . . perhaps some of us—ah, Jews, would wish to go to another town."

Margarite stares at me, expressionless.

"He says that perhaps in the larger cities the people are not so— well, I suppose you know that the rabble are on the rampage," I continue, using Closener's own words. "They believe this absurdity about the wells. That we throw poison into the water, bringing pestilence. But in Frankfurt the people are educated, and they abide by the edicts of the pope, who has told them we are blameless. In Frankfurt—"

Margarite takes a step backward, as if to escape from a snare. "What do I know of Frankfurt?" she says, her voice high pitched and trembling. "What do I know at all of anyplace but here?"

"Well, there are other places, Margarite, fine places with people who—"

"What people do I want except my family and my friends? You think I would leave them? Are you asking me to leave them, Johannes? Are you utterly mad?"

I try to change it now, squirming, lightening my tone. "I didn't mean it, Margarite. I only tell you what the man said. He knows nothing of our ways, our families. I only tell you—"

"Do not tell me these things," says Margarite. She picks up her basket and goes to the door. "Come, Rosa!" she calls.

Rosa appears, with Rochele beside her. The two little girls stand close together, solemn.

"What is it?" Margarite asks.

"Rochele told me they have burned the Jews in many places," says Rosa. "I think it would hurt to be burned."

"Rochele, keep your mouth shut!" I grasp her arm and give her a shake. "What is the matter with you, making Rosa almost cry? Those people were in Switzerland, nowhere near here. Oh, perhaps in some villages, where idiots live, far from here, in the mountains where they are all cuckoo."

Margarite nods and pulls Rosa to her. "Johannes is right," she says. "Don't think about these things."

"I heard the rabbi saying it," Rosa insists, her lower lip thrust out. "He said the people would not take the cross. I know what that means. They do not pray to Jesu, because they do not believe he is really God. I don't believe it, either. Mama explained it to me. He was a man, like any other, and we must not pray to him. But Rochele and I—we have a plan."

I look from Margarite to my little sister. I bend down toward her. "What is your plan, Rochele?"

"Well, if they come for us, to burn us," she says, laughing slightly and sliding her foot along the floor, embarrassed, "if they ask us to pray to Jesu, we say we will do it, gladly! But in truth, we will not do it. We will just say it, so they will go away."

Margarite and I hold each other's gaze. It is an intimate moment; I feel as if these little sisters are our very own children. At last I say, "It is a good idea, Rochele, but not for us. Not for us. Because we cannot lie about such things. No, *Adonai* wants us for His own, and we have promised to be His, no matter what."

"We must go," says Margarite with a nod to me and a farewell to Mother, who is spinning at the far side of the room. "*Grüss Gott.* Good health to you, Johannes." She kneels down, pulls Rochele to her, and kisses her on the lips.

I know for whom that kiss was really meant. "I will save the lemon rind for you!" I call out with quick exuberance. I am amazed and gratified. No evil in the world can touch us, for Margarite and I have this love.

CHAPTER
SEVENTEEN

I nformation comes to our community not slowly or gently, like snow drifting down, but like an avalanche. The pestilence spreads throughout Germany. It moves like a pack of wild wolves, stealthy and terrible, overtaking entire populations, devouring entire villages. Parents flee from their own children. Whole streets stand deserted, with bodies heaped in a ditch. Friend turns against friend, slamming the door and barring the windows. But for us, the fear is doubled, for we are accused.

Everyone in the Jewish section knows the peril. The people burst through the streets with terror in their eyes. They grab their children roughly, pull them and push them, as if any maneuver can make a difference. Their talk is shrill. Their silences are vast. They meet late into the night. They debate. They argue.

Zebulon, the teacher, offers reason. "They will surely realize that Jews are also dying of pestilence. How, then, can we be held responsible? Besides, there is no sickness in Strasbourg. Some towns have been spared. Maybe it will not reach us here at all."

Vivelin Rote beats his fist upon the table. "What do they care about reason? They want money. All the world revolves on gold. We must pay off the council. And when did we last give a gift to the bishop?"

We take up a collection. Father and I are forced by circumstances to contribute. The money box comes by, and I drop in a handful of silver, shuddering at my own hypocrisy. Some of the money will be used to buy a new robe with a fur lining for the bishop. Some will go to bribe the council to leave us alone.

Dovie, the shipbuilder who has not built anything in years, shouts out his objection. "It is not the church or the city but the debtors who agitate."

"We could cancel all the debts," says my father. "Will we be safe then?"

"If it is only a matter of money," ponders the rabbi. "If only that . . ."

Yes, it is a matter of money but also more than money. As the pestilence nears, the people panic. The Jews are rounded up in Solothurn, Zofingen, and Stuttgart. They are separated, kept under guard. The local people, peasants and merchants, burghers, and even the nobles, begin to murmur. "Why have we kept these Jews here? They are a curse."

"Look at them strutting about, as if they were like normal folk! They are dangerous, causing all our troubles. Heretics! Devils! We should have known by their queer looks and their queer ways; they are not like us. Did you know they are not actually human? They have hidden horns and tails."

In the towns of Solothurn, Zofingen, and Stuttgart the Jews are burned like mad dogs, like witches. The townspeople—nobles and tradesmen and peasants alike—divide up the spoils: The gentry claim the houses, and the others take what is left—furniture, clothing, jewelry, animals, and the small stores of food in bins. Everyone is satisfied, the debtors most of all, for when the lender is gone, all debts are canceled. And they have done their duty. The Jews are gone. No longer will the dreaded pestilence invade their towns. The burners congratulate themselves. Some even change their names, so that posterity will know, thus Tomas the Tall becomes Tomas Judebrenner, Burner of Jews.

The news is borne on the wind. The madness spreads swiftly to other villages and towns. Terror propels the people, and greed.

I hear these things, and I am overcome with a sense of doom that is more than foreboding; it suffocates me. I sniff the air. Perhaps the smoke of these burnings lingers. But no, in Strasbourg all is silent and serene. Now some people, like Reb Zebulon and Frau Freda, say there is nothing to fear. The bishop is pleased with his new robe.

He will protect us. How ridiculous to compare Solothurn, Zofingen, and Stuttgart to a place like Strasbourg.

In December the massacres spread. In Landsberg, Burren, Memmingen, and Lindau, the Jews are herded together and burned. Father and I no longer speak to anyone about repaying loans. We tread lightly. We keep our heads down and our collars up. Father, Grandfather, Benjamin, and I sit together late each afternoon and study. Rabbi Meier has urged everyone to redouble their studies. We must keep our hearts free and our minds clear. Rabbi Meier implores us to remember the daily prayers, not to omit a single word!

In January, we see a large number of wine casks floating down the Rhine. Benjamin and I stand among the small crowd on the riverbank, as several woodsmen pull out the casks and pry them open, hoping for booty. The casks are filled with bodies of Jews. It is a ghastly sight. Benjamin and I run home, and we shiver together in a corner. Benjamin vomits and cannot eat all the next day.

The pestilence spreads. In Freiburg, but two days' journey from Strasbourg, and in Ulm, all the Jews are murdered. The disease moves on. We hear about it from lone travelers, from families fleeing in carts. The city council meets to discuss barring the city gates.

Gunther appears at my door one day, looking like an apparition, with a hood over his head, half concealing his face. His skin is white with cold, lips pale and swollen. We stand at the side of the house, our heads close together.

"I have come to warn you," whispers Gunther. "I sweep the council chambers. I hear things."

I draw Gunther inside. It seems dangerous for us to be seen speaking together.

"Johannes, who is that with you?" cries Father in alarm, and Mother rushes over to see, throwing up her hands, exclaiming, "Gunther, what are you doing here?"

We move near the fire.

"If you please," says Gunther, pulling off his hat and twisting it in his hands, "I have but come to warn you. Johannes is my friend. I hear talk of their intentions. Mother said to warn you."

"Sit down, lad," says Father. His face is mottled, eyes hooded from lack of sleep. "We are thankful that you would come to us. But what can you tell us that we do not know? We have heard about the other communities."

Grandfather sits rocking himself and humming a strange song, perhaps something from his youth. His gaze is vague.

"Well, sir," Gunther begins, wetting his lips nervously, "the town council has been called to a meeting in Benfeld. Leaders from all the states of Alsace are going, and also the bishop."

"Yes? Yes?" Father prompts him. "What is the meeting about?"

"They are meeting to . . . to discuss the . . . the Jewish question. Our Peter Swarber received a message from the council of Köln. They said things are getting very bad." Again Gunther wets his lips. "They said the Jews are being burned everywhere, and that things are getting out of hand. If the rabble go and burn the Jew houses, the fire could spread to the whole town. So they are having this meeting to decide."

"Decide what?" asks Father, and I echo his words. "What, Gunther?"

"Well, they want to decide whether the Jews have really been poisoning the wells in Alsace. And if they have, maybe they should be burned right off—and not wait until the pestilence strikes."

"When is this meeting?" Father asks.

"On Sunday next."

"Thank you, Gunther. Thank you for telling us."

"Mother says it is the least we can do, as you have been kind to us and—"

"Yes. Thank you." Father rises and walks with Gunther to the door. I clasp Gunther's hand and thank him, too. Gunther's steps are heavy as he starts to walk away. But he turns. "Oh, one thing more," he says.

"Yes?" Father and I stand at the door, impatient to close off the cold.

"Herr Swarber says the streets of the Jews must be barricaded and the Jews kept under watch."

"When?" I ask, a croak, a rasping sound.

"I think starting tomorrow," says Gunther, his shoulders hunched, warming his hands under his armpits. "Tomorrow night."

Barricade. It is the beginning. First they will separate us, keep us under guard, and then . . . There is a time for action. I know this from my Torah study. When God parted the Red Sea so that the Jews could escape from the Egyptian cavalry, Moses stood on the banks, weeping and praying. And God chided him: "Why do you stand there praying? Move out! Go!"

Calmly I ask my mother, "Where is Benjamin?"

Mother is moving bowls and mugs and spoons from one shelf to another. She opens bins and boxes, shuffles things about. Her cap is askew. She flounders, like a messenger without a message.

"He is with the rabbi, learning."

"I will go and get him," I say.

"Hurry," says Father. "It is nearly dark."

"I'll hurry, Father," I promise. As I go, the plan becomes complete in my mind. It has been smoldering in my thoughts for weeks.

I hurry up the street where Dr. Yunge lives. Only a few people are about, hurrying home for the evening prayers. At the doctor's house I knock loudly. Immediately Jacob appears. The old doctor is asleep in the corner, collapsed in a heap amid several large cushions.

"What is it?" Jacob whispers. "You look as if—"

"They are barricading our streets tomorrow night." I gasp. "If you are going to leave—"

"What are you saying?"

"You have said you want to go to Frankfurt. If it is what you want, you must go now, before it is too late. You know very well, if they put up a barricade, nobody will be allowed in or out."

Jacob stands stock-still, staring. He seems not even to be breathing, except that his chest rises and falls. His face becomes flooded with deep color.

"Go at dawn," I say. "Wear as many clothes as you can." I look at Jacob's feet. "You have boots. That's good. Take off the Jew hat. You have a cloak with a hood, you have your satchel. Anyone could take you for a Muslim with that black beard of yours. And with your medical bag, you could well be a Muslim doctor."

"What are you saying? That I should—"

"Go to Frankfurt. Tend the sick there."

"But . . . what about . . . Will you come with me?" Jacob clasps my shoulders. "Come with me, Johannes! Why should you stay? You can be my assistant. You can—"

"No. It is out of the question. You know it, Jacob."

"Well, I can't go alone. I won't. And the roads—"

"The roads are good enough," I say, "for a man on a horse."

"A horse," repeats Jacob. He starts to laugh. "Who has a horse?"

"My brother, Benjamin, has a horse."

"I wouldn't know how to handle it."

"Leave it to me," I tell him.

That evening, as we eat our supper of mutton and bread and ale, I notice every small detail, memorizing the moments. The way the fire flickers, the small giggle from Rochele, the sleepy nods of Grandfather, whose eyes are dull and untroubled—I will remember this. Benjamin speaks through most of the meal about Rabbi Meier and the things he has learned. He speaks of becoming a teacher, perhaps a traveling teacher; and of course, Matilda is part of his plans. I notice how Father bends over his bowl, eating awkwardly with his left hand. He and Mother exchange a quiet look, deep and trusting. Mother shakes her head slightly, as if to say, "Let him talk, let him dream, he is just a boy."

At night, when the others are asleep, I go to Benjamin's pallet. "Benjamin! Listen to me. Say nothing, just listen!"

Benjamin sits up, instantly awake and alert. "What is it?" Benjamin whispers. Moonlight through the window shines upon my brother's face.

Swiftly I explain, ending, "So you can take Jacob on Matilda. She is strong enough, isn't she, for two?"

"Of course," Benjamin says stoutly. "She's a fine, strong animal. But what about Mother and Father? They won't let me go."

"Go before dawn, when nobody can stop you, nobody will see you. Don't worry, Benjamin. Leave it to me."

"What if I am questioned along the way? What shall I say?"

Already I hold the knife in my hand. "They will not think you are a Jew," I say, cutting off the long curl at Benjamin's temple. "Wear Grandfather's old black cloak. You can carry a bag. I have one here for you. With those peasant's hands of yours, nobody would take you for a Jew. And with that horse, you look like a Muslim. You will be the doctor's assistant."

Just after daybreak, Mother scuttles around the room, sniffing like a fox whose prey has been stolen, whose lair is defiled. "Where is your brother?" she asks.

I go to her. I hold out my hands to her. "Mother, listen. Jacob needed to go to Frankfurt. A doctor there has sent for him. Benjamin has taken him there on the horse. It is a good thing for Benjamin to help Jacob. Benjamin was glad to go, Mother. He wanted an adventure."

Mother gasps. "You allowed this? You made this decision?" Her face is deep red, her eyes wide and flashing.

"Everything pointed to this outcome, Mother," I say. Each word is measured, firm, as I have practiced it through the night. "Whoever thought we would have a horse? Whoever thought that pathetic horse would even survive? It was all meant to be—Jacob returning to us here, and now having this calling to Frankfurt, now when we face a barricade, questions, meetings . . ."

Rochele comes close, rubbing her eyes. "Where is Frankfurt?" she asks. "Is it in France?"

I answer my little sister, but my eyes are still on my mother's stricken face. "Frankfurt is a large city, Rochele, filled with many different kinds of people who do not know us. Jacob is going there to work with a doctor, and Benjamin has taken him on Matilda, because that is the best way, the safest way to go."

"When will Benjamin be back?" Rochele wants to know.

"Soon," says Mother, blinking rapidly. "When God wills."

CHAPTER
EIGHTEEN

The streets of the Jews are barricaded now. Guards stand at every intersection. Their eyes are dagger sharp; their jaws firm. We may walk past them, but we do not speak or meet their gaze. It is the unwritten rule for the captive.

Amid the prison atmosphere, news still travels. News comes in from the miller, from the midwife, from Greta the Winker milking cows, from all sources, creating fuel for the frenzy of talk. Rabbi Meier holds meetings at his house nearly every night.

Brazenly the debtors come, beating on our door. "We have come to take back our pledges," they say.

"But . . . you have not yet repaid the debt!"

"No matter." A smile, leering and conspiratorial. "Times have changed."

Father and I stand helplessly by as the debtors stride boldly through our room, taking back rings, cloaks, swords, and armor. We dare not object. It would mean trouble for everyone. I feel like a coward as I stand beside Father, seeing the whiteness of his countenance. I know that he is trembling from both fear and rage.

Some of the men led by Dovie, the shipbuilder, hold secret meetings in the night. They are planning resistance. They have gathered a small cache of arms: knives and swords, cudgels, and even slingshots.

Vivelin Rote's mansion is filled with visitors coming and going. He has paid the bishop's taxes in advance; he has paid the nobles their due and offered a large donation to complete the east tower of the new abbey. Bribery is not new to us; we will buy our lives if we must.

Margarite and I meet every day just outside the bathhouse in the nearby garden, which is now winter white. An arbor waits like a bony skeleton, robbed of the flowers that clothed it during summer.

We stand close together, still without touching, and I am wrapped in longing and regret and a peculiar happiness. Everything matters. The smallest leaf drifting from the tree, the single chortle of a sparrow, the track of a raccoon, the trickle of icy water rushing down over the glittering stones—everything is a wonder.

I tell her about Benjamin, that I sent him away. She says, "He will be witness for us."

"What do you mean?" I ask. I miss my brother terribly; without him, there is a hole in the house.

Margarite's lips form a slight, wise smile, as if she already knows the future. "He will tell everything," she says, "to the world. Then they will not forget."

I tell Margarite about my dream. I cannot escape the dark dreams that torment me. They come more and more often, and linger into the day. "Last night," I say, "I dreamed of a place where people were not allowed to tell stories or to talk about the past. There was no history."

She says, "A strange dream, Johannes. Without history, how can there be any meaning?"

"It was so vivid, this dream! Love was forbidden. So was music."

"Love and music," she muses. "They go together."

"Yes," I say. "I love you, Margarite. You and my music."

"It is because you love your music so much," Margarite says, "that you had this dream. You have many loves."

"Many? No," I say. "Not many, only you."

"But you must count your friends and your family," Margarite reminds me. "And then also the love of God."

How fortunate I am! I take out my flute and play, but softly. Passersby would think me insane to play at such a time as this, with menace everywhere. But with Margarite I feel happiness, and a kind of peace. No matter what happens, we are together.

Margarite sometimes brings Rosa out to play in the snow, and I bring Rochele. We make snowballs, a snow house, snowmen, a snow dog! The little girls wear mittens and cloaks; they are bundled into layers of clothing, looking round and funny. Sometimes they stumble in the snow and slide down the icy banks. Then they giggle, and Margarite laughs with them and warms their hands. She would be a wonderful mother.

I think constantly of Benjamin. I try to imagine how it was for him along the way, with Jacob and the horse. Were people kind? Or are he and Jacob cold and hungry?

On Sunday, February 8, in Benfeld, the meeting is held. The great feudal lords, all the town leaders, and the Bishop Berthold of Strasbourg sit in heavy discussion. They clamor and argue. Peter Swarber denies that the Jews of Strasbourg are guilty of any wrong-doing. He is adamant. Leave them alone!

The others mock him, shouting, "If they are blameless, then why have you covered your wells?" They hardly allow him the chance to answer. He speaks of precautions against pollutants; it has nothing to do with Jews or with poison. But they laugh at him and they vote. *Guilty.* All this I hear from Gunther, who comes through the back lanes to see me each evening. I meet him under the trees, thick with shadows.

Father implores me, "Don't go out, Johannes! Stay inside with us!"

"I must go, Father," I tell him. "I must know the truth."

Gunther is my link, now, to the greater world. Whatever truth he tells me, it is better than lies, better than ignorance. I must be prepared.

On Monday, February 9, the guild members of Strasbourg meet. Their leaders present the questions: "What shall we do with the Jews? Our Councilman, Swarber, says they are innocent. What do you think? What do you say?"

They say, "Guilty." They march, each guild under its own banner—the tanners, the bakers, the tilers, and the butchers. Oh, what a day! The chill of winter is gentled by a sudden layer of sunshine, which glazes the frost and makes it shine. The streets are slick with runoff. Cobblestones gleam blue and gray and tan. Animals frisk in that peculiar pleasure signifying the first inkling of another spring.

The guild members march, battle-bound, along the streets, past the very streets of the Jews, straight to the door of Peter Swarber, councilman. The butcher, Betscholt, speaks for them all.

"Peter Swarber, come out! Show your face!"

Bishop Berthold stands to one side, snug in his new fur robe. The bishop gives the butcher a nod. Peter Swarber has been a thorn in his side. The councilmen do not show him proper respect, nor do they turn over enough tax money for his wishes.

A crowd has gathered now, peasants and burghers, merchants and paupers. They shout and cheer. "A new council! Elect strong men who will do the right thing!"

The mob hurls stones against Peter Swarber's house. Swarber comes out, shaken. "You take bribes from the Jews," accuses Betscholt, pointing, "to let them live. Why else would you protect them?"

"Jew lover!" screams the crowd. "Get him out! We don't need his kind here."

Gunther tells me that, late that night, Peter Swarber left town. All his possessions—his house, his horses, and his furniture were left standing. Swarber's possessions are divided among the guild leaders. Finally, the mob descends on his house, picking up the few remnants within—a cracked mirror, an old barrel, a cleaver.

On Tuesday, February 10, a new council is elected. The new council boasts men who are tough and unsentimental. The position held by Peter Swarber is given to the butcher, Betscholt.

On Wednesday, February 11, the old council members leave town in great haste. The rabble pursues them, shouting warnings. They are not to return to Strasbourg for ten years. Their goods are given away.

On Thursday, February 12, in the garden by the great guild hall, the new council is sworn in. Included are Count Engelbracht and the nobleman Zorn.

On Friday, February 13, a small army of magistrates comes to arrest the Jews. I hear them coming down the street.

Rochele is wearing her Sabbath dress, with blue ribbons in her hair. Mother has finished cooking; a large pot of soup with vegetables and dumplings is warming in the coals. Father has bathed himself and combed his hair. Grandfather sits in a chair, nodding, staring without seeing. His fingers rub and twitch constantly.

I go through the house like a miser, counting our possessions. It is not that mere things mean much to me, but each item holds a memory. There is Grandmother's shawl, Mother's prized blue bowls, Father's pledge box, Benjamin's book, Rochele's small doll with one eye missing. I see Grandfather's walking staff, the handle he carved out many years ago. I stare at the table where we always eat and study and pray. Our things—our things are extensions of our own selves. What if some stranger put his hands upon them?

I keep my flute in my pocket. I will not let it out of my sight. And as the magistrates make their way along the street, I am drawn to the window. I hold the flute to my lips. The wedding song comes into my mind, and I am filled with so many feelings that only music can express them. The music weeps and sings, it mourns and praises; the music is longing and regret, love and hope. Whatever happens to me, whatever happens in the world, music has a life and a meaning of its own.

I play the wedding song over and over again as the magistrates come down the street, gathering their captives. The magistrates march all in a line, swinging their arms and thrusting out their feet. They pound on doors and burst in without waiting to be met.

"Jews! Out!"

From along the street I hear cries and murmurs. "Where to? Where are you taking us? What have we done?"

"Jews! Out!"

There is a skirmish. It does not last long. Dovie and his defenders are dragged along the streets. There are howls, almost inhuman, then silence. Blood streaks the road and stains the snow. The bodies lie there, indecently sprawled.

"Come along!" yell the magistrates. They have gathered Dovie's knives and swords together. "Hurry."

"Wait, please, let me take—"

"You will need nothing."

"The children!"

"The children, too."

"Where are you taking us?"

"To the towers. Come, come. Hurry!"

Rabbi Meier is shouting. His sons plead and gesture and throw themselves down before the magistrates. "At least," they cry, "at least let us prepare ourselves. It is almost the Sabbath. We must bring our prayer books and our Sabbath wine for blessing."

The magistrates laugh and nudge one another. They kick up their heels. "Yes, yes, bring your things, then."

"Have your Sabbath," the chief magistrate says. " 'Tis a witches' Sabbath."

Rabbi Meier shouts again. "Grant us one request, then. Tomorrow let musicians be brought. Let musicians play glad songs, so that we can go with rejoicing."

The magistrates look at one another, amazed and amused. One slaps his thigh. "Music. Yes. You can go with music."

Mother begins to scramble for bread, for cups and bowls. "Johannes! Quick, lift the kettle from the fire. We will take it with us. We must have food."

How like Mother to think of food, to know that an empty stomach is the devil's own curse, making bad things worse, as the saying goes. I hoist the kettle down and hold it at my side.

Mother is panting. "Rochele, where are the candles? Quick, take them, and the holders, too."

The magistrates are pounding at the door. "Come out! Immediately!"

I run to open the door, lest they break it. "We are coming!" I shout. I pull Rochele by the hand, holding tight.

Why do we go so obediently? I could grasp a knife and plunge it swiftly into the magistrate's throat. Perchance I could push my way through and run. Where would I go that they would not catch me? We are outnumbered, caught like foxes pursued by hounds.

Rochele gives a little cry. She pulls away from me and rushes back to snatch up her box of pressed flowers. "Rochele!" I scream.

Mother plucks up an extra shawl and throws it over Grandfather's shoulders.

Grandfather tucks the Sabbath loaf under his arm. We do not look back but leave the door wide open as the magistrates storm behind us, shouting, "Hurry! Hurry! What is all this nonsense? Come along, now—what a fuss!"

It is cold and the sky is gray and dusky with clouds. Nobody speaks as we move along the canal, past the silent houses, to the watchtowers, which rise tall and dark against the late afternoon sky. The only sounds are those of water lapping gently against the quay, and the shuffle of many feet, and an occasional shout. "Hurry!"

Inside, we are crammed together. The huge iron doors are slammed shut and bolted from the outside.

We find one another—friends, relatives. Margarite's family and mine cling together. Rosa's and Rochele's arms are wound around each other's waists. Never have I seen two little girls act so kindly toward each other. Rosa is telling Rochele, "Do not be afraid—here, I have brought you a sweet. Take it."

It takes some time and shuffling about; then there is a settling. Women light their Sabbath candles; they lift their hands, encircling the glowing flames, and recite the Sabbath prayers. Those who have brought wine share with others. The cup is passed to me, and I drink and hold the sweetness in my mouth for a long moment.

Somehow the night passes. We eat the Sabbath bread. The soup is cold. It does not matter. Margarite and I sit together. We share a piece of bread; we eat from one bowl, taking turns, so that I can watch her as she eats. With every mouthful my heart surges toward her, and I want to say, "Eat, my love! Be strong and live."

"I feel as if we are married," Margarite whispers to me. There is a flush on her cheeks; it spreads to her whole face.

"Then this is our wedding night," I whisper.

"Play the wedding song," she says.

"I cannot," I remind her. "It is Sabbath, when instruments are forbidden."

"But we can sing," says she.

We hum the tune. Soon other voices join ours. And then the entire tower is rocked with songs of Sabbath praise and Sabbath joy; and the many candles cast their golden glow upon the tower walls.

It grows late. Children sleep. Their parents doze. Now and again someone wakes with a cry.

"Do not sleep," I urge Margarite. "Let us stay awake together."

Margarite agrees, and we talk, remembering all the days that we can. Each small thing that seemed insignificant now stands clear and cherished.

"Remember the day we went to the meadows? How we danced?"

"Remember last Yom Kippur, how warm it was, and the flowers still blooming on the hillsides?"

"Remember the snowman we made just the other day?"

We tell not only our own stories, but stories of the sages and the martyrs, of Reb Akiba, of Hanna and her seven sons, all now in the Garden of Eden, all blessed and revered.

"What will happen?" Rochele asks again and again. Mother caresses her. She and Father sit close together, holding hands. Grandfather has rocked himself to sleep. He awakens now and then, muttering, "Run! Run!"

"What will happen to us, Mama?"

"We don't know, Rochele."

At last I take Rochele to my side. Rosa is fast asleep in her father's arms. "Look, you are a big girl, Rochele," I tell her. "You are my sister. We will be together tomorrow and always, all of us, you and Rosa, Margarite and me, Mother and Father and Grandfather, and the entire community. We are one."

"Are they taking us to the forest to be eaten by wolves?" Rochele shudders and shakes. "I would hate to be eaten by wolves, Johannes! Don't let them take me."

"You will be safe from wolves, Rochele, I promise you. When it is time to go, I will hold your hand. We will sing, you and I. We will sing very loudly, for everyone to hear our voices. Now go to sleep." I put my arm around her. Her head is on my chest. "You must be in good voice for tomorrow."

We are silent for a time. I think only of escape, of freedom. Who is really free? There must be rules. But who should make them? In the Passover story we learn that we were freed from being slaves to Pharaoh, so that we could be servants of God.

Margarite whispers, "What are you thinking about, Johannes?"

"I am thinking about Benjamin, hoping he is free. That he can walk wherever he will, that he can talk to anyone he meets and be respected."

"That sounds like paradise," says Margarite. "In this world, somebody is always brought low."

"But listen!" I bend toward her, suddenly alert. "You were the one who talked about changing the world. What if there were no Jew hats, no badges, no hatred? Everyone could follow his own ways and come together to . . ." My mind races over possibilities and I recall that afternoon with Closener, when the two of us were joined in spirit. "People would come together," I say, "to make music. And after that, talk."

"It would be paradise," Margarite admits. "What would we have to do? We would have to change, too. We would really have to love everyone—gentiles, nobles, priests, and even lepers."

I ponder this. "Even lepers. Yes."

I cannot remain awake all night, however hard I try. Beside me, Margarite is sleeping, too. I dream of a strange clinic, and of people wearing golden masks. Again the masks—am I going mad? I almost laugh to myself. Does it matter now whether anyone is sane anymore or not?

In the morning everything is brittle and dry. Throats are parched. There is no water. We wait, hungry and cold and frightened. Children whimper. Mother takes my hand; she holds it very tight. I want to say so many things to her, but no words come. There is this very strange sense of isolation, yet also of a profound togetherness.

I hear people speaking, and their words seem oddly disconnected.

"Maybe one of the councilmen . . ."

"Maybe the bishop . . ."

"Maybe even the pope . . ."

"Maybe a miracle will save us."

At last the tower doors are flung open. People push against one another. I want to scream, but I grit my teeth. Rochele, Mother, and

I hold on to one another. Rabbi Meier climbs up on a bench and calls out, "Order! Be calm, my friends. Come. We go together."

Outside we blink against the sudden light. The day is breezy. There are clouds in the sky, among bright patches of blue. The air is cold and fresh in the lungs. It revives me. I look up and breathe deep, and the fresh, clear air brings a strange exultation into my entire body and soul. I tell Rochele, "Breathe deep! Deep!"

Now, as we walk, I hear music. Music accompanies us as we move, flanked by magistrates. "Hurry! Hurry!" they shout, prodding the stragglers with their clubs. "Hurry!" Still the musicians play their instruments, harmonica and hurdy-gurdy, trumpet and tambourine, flute and fiddle and drum.

It is a spectacle! All along the streets the people have assembled, and as they catch sight of us, they shout and scream and jeer, their voices rising louder than any multitude that has ever gathered here before. Occasionally one darts out to grasp at a gown or a kerchief, ripping it, looking for possible jewels or gold hidden there.

I see fathers holding up babies to witness the march. A mother pulls her daughter roughly around, gives her a sharp slap, shouting, "Look! Look! I want you to remember this, what is done to heretics!"

Several men shout obscenely, "Give her to me, that comely one! Perchance she will save herself. I shall baptize her myself! What a beauty—pity for such a one to be burned."

All the while, the music plays, louder, faster. I grasp Rochele, holding her tight, and in my other hand is my flute. Music rings in my ears—peasant songs, marching songs, festive songs—and suddenly I hear the tune I learned at Troyes. Fritsche Closener is with the musicians, playing his recorder, playing so loudly that his face is red and his eyes look ready to burst from their sockets. The song ends. And now we begin to sing. It starts softly at first, gathering strength like a winter storm, resounding like thunder:

> *"I believe in the coming of* Moshiach!
> *And though he may tarry,*
> *Still I await him every day . . ."*

I throw back my head, thrust out my chest, and I sing. I hear Rochele beside me, singing, singing. Mother stumbles; Father half carries her along. All around me people stagger. Some fall, some are dazed. Moshe the Bent is limping and holding his shoulder where a stone has nicked him, hard. Frau Freda has lost her cap, and she covers her head with her hands. Elias and Chava catch each other around the waist. Rosa clings to her father's arm. Chava holds her bodice together where it has been shamefully ripped. The baker holds a small child on each arm. His wife is pregnant; her swollen belly makes her sway.

Rochele's fingernails dig into my wrist. Margarite runs up beside us. I take her hand. It is very cold. I press her fingers.

"I believe in the coming of *Moshiach!*"

There are screams now, as the spectators rush at us. They try to tear rings from people's fingers, the jewels from women's ears. A man snatches a baby from its mother, and a woman screams, "I will baptize thee!"

"Give me the baby! Give me my child!"

Now, in the blur, I begin to see faces of people I know. There is the miller who grinds wheat for the Jews. There is the wine maker and the tavern girl. There is Gunther, stricken, white with shock. He rushes up to me.

I press the flute into his hands. "Take it, take it!" I cry.

Greta strides into the melee. She grasps Rochele's arm and calls out, "Let me take her. I will raise her. Let me . . ."

"Mother!" Rochele screams. "Mother!"

Mother, her face ashen, opens her hand and smacks Greta the Winker on the side of the head. "Leave her! She is my child."

Greta falls back. "Mistress, I beg you. Let me take her. I am a mother, too. I will tend her. They will baptize her; she can be saved. I will raise her like my own."

"No!"

The crowd surges on, and the magistrates, fearful now of a riot, prod the Jews with sticks and cudgels and whips. "Hurry! Hurry!"

The cemetery gates are wide open. Sodden patches of snow

surround the tombstones with their Hebrew engravings. Some have lain here for a hundred years.

"Hurry! Hurry!"

Still the music plays, but now that we are here—at the very edge of the pit, standing all around the scaffolding that has been built expressly for this purpose—the crowd falls silent. Only the music plays on and on.

It plays as we are pushed onto the scaffolding, where wood is piled into a pyramid. It plays as the twigs are laid all around, all around. It plays as the torches are brought forth—huge, blazing torches—to ignite the sticks that will blaze up into a leaping furnace.

I try to look past the flames and smoke. I cannot breathe. I cannot speak. My eyes fill. But I glimpse the face of Konrad, the hair pale as straw, mouth wide open in amazed disbelief. It is as if the very words are written on Konrad's face, along with his tears: *I never thought, never intended, never knew . . .*

The music plays.

And the fire grows.

And the smoke obliterates everything from my eyes, except a single patch of blue sky. I gaze at it continually.

Rochele is screaming uncontrollably.

Where is everyone? Where is the world? I am drowning in the fierce, hot, unbearable pain. I hear others cry out the eternal words; I join them. My entire being is given to the prayer: "*Shema Yisroel . . .* Hear, oh Israel . . . the Lord is one."

And in that last moment, I feel the arms of my love around my entire body, warm and soft. I call out to her, "Fly with me. I'm flying!"

Then I am merged into the music.

CHAPTER NINETEEN

UNITED SOCIAL ALLIANCE, WESTERN SECTOR:
The Year of Tranquillity 2407

He's coming out of it now."

"Turn up the music."

"Easy. Hold his arms. He's a bit wild."

Technicians and Elders crowd around, peering at Gemm 16884. He struggles. He lets out a bloodcurdling scream. "Stop! Stop! I beg you, stop the music!"

An Elder motions for the music to linger. He watches intently as Gemm 16884 writhes, his hands covering his ears, his eyes streaming with tears as he continues to plead, "Stop the music. Please."

"You don't want the music?" asks the Elder. His tone is stern.

"No! I beg you, let me not hear music anymore. Never again! Never again!"

"What happens with music, Gemm 16884? What does music release?"

Gemm 16884 feels the throbbing in his head. He gasps for breath. "It . . . it releases passion. Anger and evil and death! I felt . . . such pain; and the music played. The music—oh, I pray you, let it never sound again!"

"How were the people?" the Elder persists. He is surrounded by many others, all wearing the golden masks and the royal blue jumpers. "Were the people in harmony? Were they in conformity?"

"I . . . I am ashamed to speak of it," Gemm whispers. "It was so . . . diverse. People believed just as they wished. They behaved—oh, without restraint. It was horrible! Horrible! You can't imagine what they did to each other."

"Tell us," commands the Elder. "Tell us everything."

"It was . . . chaos and killing and . . ." Gemm cannot bear to think of it. He covers his mask with his hands to blot out the vision. He opens his eyes, takes in the white brilliance of sanitized light, breathes in the pure, scented air. "I never knew," he whispers, "how beautiful this is—the harmony, the conformity—how perfect and true!"

The Elders nod. Their golden masks gleam, and as one they intone the mantra. Gemm 16884 lifts his voice with theirs: "Conformity begets Harmony begets Tranquillity begets Peace begets Universal Good. Shout praises!"

A great shout of praise fills the room, and Gemm feels a new burst of strength and resolve. He stands, feeling tall and perfect, cleansed. "Can you ever forgive me for . . . for my deviance?"

Three Elders confer. They stand close together, gazing at the hologram, at Gemm's life chart. They bid him stand in the recessed figure; and as the mechanism scans and blinks and finally settles into the projection that now represents Gemm 16884, they breathe a collective sigh. The Chief Elder strides out from among the others.

"Gemm 16884," he calls out loudly, "we declare you cured. Furthermore, having accepted and survived The Cure, having endured pain and suffering, you now understand that only by the teachings of our United Social Alliance can we survive."

"Yes. It is true." Gemm bows his head in humility.

"You understand that outside the group of Revered Elders, you must never speak to anyone of The Cure. Is this agreed?"

"In love, it is agreed."

The Elder continues, "Indeed, this experience will swiftly fade from your memory, like a bad dream. Also, serotonin replacement and the other supplements will soon take effect, and you will be as before. Only now, you will be utterly content and committed to our work."

"In love, I thank you."

Gemm 16884 is led to a decompression lounge, where Gemma 16884 waits for him. She is wearing a glad mask of pale yellow, with beautiful blue hair, and a smile that never dims.

Gemma tells Gemm events of the day gone by—the amusements,

the lectures and Folk Facts, the serotonin flavors, the games, puzzles, and conversations. She speaks of Kir and Kira, Zo and Zoa, and all the others who asked about him and were merely told he was in convalescence. He nods and listens. He feels as if he is floating at the very top of the universe, glancing down at an ant heap, where tiny creatures go about their tiny lives, completely unaware of any force or future outside themselves.

They spend a day in reunion, with food and pictures and sweet scented breezes—with hologram games and experiences. Meanwhile, the Elders sit in meeting. They discuss the question of Gemm, his future.

At last they send for Gemm and Gemma 16884. In the large chamber many Elders are seated in a semicircle, attentive, waiting. Gemm and Gemma are led to the podium, where the Chief Elder stands, ready to deliver his edict.

He speaks. "Gemm 16884, we, the Committee of Revered Elders, have reached agreement. You and your twin are hereby given new status. Are you willing, Gemm 16884, to be advanced to the apprenticeship of Elder? Are you willing to accept the honor and the responsibility for preserving all that we hold so dear?"

Gemm lifts his head. He feels exalted and breathless. "In love," he says, "I am willing." None of his peers have been so honored. He is overwhelmed.

"Your twin, naturally, will join you in the course of study. Your rehabilitation is complete, but you must learn exactly how the Elders maintain this exalted state of society, where nobody need fear harm or violence, where life is pure and good and harmonious. We believe that you are now capable of such heights. Are you willing to attain them?"

"Indeed! Indeed I am," exclaims Gemm. And as he stands, surrounded by Elders, he can imagine his entire life—the full span of 120 years—being lived in the daily certainty that never will passion or diversity be allowed to violate this peace.

CHAPTER
TWENTY

UNITED SOCIAL ALLIANCE, WESTERN SECTOR:
Later that same Year of Tranquillity 2407

Their lives are orderly and predictable. Day follows day in unremarkable sequence. Night after night, with Gemma lying beside him, Gemm knows he ought to be content, but somehow sleep eludes him. When he does sleep, his dreams are deep and shattering. He dreams of a hole, a gigantic hole ripped into the universe, an emptiness that can never be filled. And he feels a great hunger and thirst that no amount of food can satisfy. Then his dreams take shape. Faces appear, words come to him, and a certain song plays in his mind over and over again.

The Elder was wrong. The memories do not fade. In fact, they grow more vivid and more demanding every day. Gemm is different. There is no denying it; he is truly diverse. And now he begins to wonder whether this is not how he is meant to be, for some reason that he cannot fathom.

One night, when Gemm is lying wide awake with Gemma sleeping beside him, a thought comes upon him with overwhelming clarity. *Maybe we can change it. Maybe we can change the world.* The idea absorbs Gemm utterly.

All night he lies awake asking himself, How? How can we stop the hate and still keep the love?

He does not know.

Near dawn, he turns and sees Gemma sleeping beside him.

Superimposed upon her masked face are the dear faces: Mother, Father, Benjamin, Rochele, Uncle David, and his own beloved Margarite. Now—distant at first, then closer and clearer—he hears the song:

Sing to the groom,
Oh, happy hearts,
Sing to the bride and groom
For as he comes, so too shall he
For whom we've waited long. . . .

For a few moments Gemm lies there on the antigravity bed, straining to understand. It comes to him all at once, an explosion of certainty.

He turns to Gemma, awakens her gently. "Gemma," he whispers. "Listen to me. I have indeed been cured."

Sleepily she murmurs, "I know, my twin, and I am so happy. I was terribly afraid that I would lose you."

He says, "Gemma, you must trust me. I will tell you everything about where I have been and what I have learned. The world is— the world can be . . ." He does not have words for it yet, nor is his plan fully formed. But he knows how it must begin. He says, "I am going to teach you a song."

"But it is forbidden," Gemma says.

"No," Gemm tells her. "I allow it. We need it, Gemma. Trust me."

Softly Gemm begins to sing.

"Sing to the groom
Oh, happy hearts,
Sing to the bride and groom,
For as he comes, so too shall he
For whom we've waited long."

Gemm sings the wedding song, verse by verse. Joy and love overwhelm him as never before in this place.

Gemma gazes at him, scarcely breathing. She whispers, "It is beautiful, my twin. But I don't understand the words. What is a bride and groom? What is a happy heart?"

Gemm 16884 sighs deeply. "How can you understand," he says softly, "until you know what love is? Until you have known pain?"

Gemma 16884 puts her hands over her ears. Gently Gemm draws her hands away. "I have been in a place," he says, "where people showed strong feelings. It was allowed. Diversity was allowed in everything. People wore no masks."

"No masks!"

"It is true that diversity leads to emotion. And emotions can bring us either to hatred or to love. People must have that choice. Do you understand?"

Gemma plucks at several strands of blue silk hair. "I am trying; but, Gemm, we already have a thousand choices."

"There is only one choice that really matters," says Gemm, "choosing what we will believe."

Gemma lies silent.

"Let me teach you," Gemm says tenderly. "Take off your mask."

"It is forbidden!"

"I allow it."

"I am afraid."

"There is much to fear, Gemma, I know. Be brave. Take it off now, and I will do the same."

Slowly, with trembling fingers, Gemma lifts her mask.

"It will begin with us," says Gemm, pulling the mask from his face and breathing deeply this new, uncluttered air. "I will teach you. Then you and I will teach others. We will teach them about love."

EPILOGUE

In the wake of the Black Death in Europe, from 1348 to 1349, thousands of Jews were killed, having been accused of poisoning the wells and bringing the pestilence. Some three hundred Jewish communities were utterly destroyed.

According to the *Encyclopedia Judaica*, on Saturday, February 14, 1349, "The Jews of Strasbourg were burnt on a wooden scaffold in the Jewish cemetery. . . . They asked the town leaders to permit them to prepare themselves for martyrdom. . . . They asked that musicians be hired to play dancing tunes so that they could enter the presence of God with singing."

These events were recorded by Fritsche Closener, a historian who lived in Strasbourg at that time. One person, a Jewish doctor named Jacob, was documented as a survivor of the Strasbourg community, living in Frankfurt some twenty years later.

Ironically, the plague did not reach Strasbourg until several weeks after the Jews had been killed. When the inhabitants of the town realized that eliminating the Jews offered no protection against the plague, few expressed remorse or altered their thinking. Throughout the Middle Ages, anti-Semitism remained so deeply ingrained in many Europeans that it led to the murder or forced conversion of thousands of Jews. In this century, when Hitler seized control of Germany in the 1930s, he was easily able to rekindle old prejudices and to proceed with the systematic murder of six million Jews and other "undesirable elements" of society.

To this very day, unfounded hatred and fear of one group against another causes untold suffering, and no one seems immune.

BIBLIOGRAPHY

Abrahams, Israel. *Jewish Life in the Middle Ages*. Philadelphia: The Jewish Publication Society of America, 1911.

Bayard, Tania, ed. and trans. *A Medieval Home Companion: Housekeeping in the Fourteenth Century*. New York: HarperCollins, 1991.

Black, Maggie. *The Medieval Cookbook*. London: British Museum Press, 1992.

"Black Death." In *Encyclopedia Judaica*. Vol. 4. Macmillan: pp. 1063–1068.

Glaser, A. *Geschichte der Juden in Strassburg*. Frankfurt am Main: J. Kaufman Verlag, 1925.

Goetz, Hans-Werner. *Life in the Middle Ages: From the Seventh to the Thirteenth Century*. Notre Dame, Ind.: University of Notre Dame Press, 1993.

Gottfried, Robert S. *The Black Death: Natural and Human Disaster in Medieval Europe*. New York: The Free Press, 1983.

Grayzel, Solomon. *A History of the Jews: From the Babylonian Exile to the Present*. Philadelphia: Jewish Publication Society, 1947.

Katz, Jacob. *Exclusiveness and Tolerance: Studies in Jewish-Gentile Relations in Medieval and Modern Times*. New York: Schocken Books, 1961.

Kieckhefer, Richard. *Magic in the Middle Ages*. Cambridge, England: Cambridge University Press, 1989.

Kisch, Guido. *The Jews in Medieval Germany: A Study of Their Legal and Social Status*. Chicago: University of Chicago Press, 1949.

Manchester, William. *A World Lit Only by Fire: The Medieval Mind and the Renaissance*. Boston: Little, Brown & Company, 1992.

Marcus, Jacob R. "Confession of Agimet of Geneva, Chatel, Oct. 10, 1348." In *The Jew in the Medieval World: A Sourcebook, 315–1791*. New York: Harper Torchbooks, 1965: pp. 43–47.

Nirenberg, David. *Communities of Violence: Persecution of Minorities in the Middle Ages*. Princeton, N.J.: Princeton University Press, 1996.

Peacock, John. *Costume, 1066–1990's*. New York: Thames and Hudson, 1994.

Rowling, Marjorie. *Life in Medieval Times*. New York: Putnam, 1968.

Strassburg und die Judenverfolgung 1348–49. Zusammengestellt unter Bearbeitet von: Lic hil. Christop Duntert. Reprint, Zurich: Aytun Altindal 1991.

Trachtenberg, Joshua. *The Devil and the Jews: The Medieval Conception of the Jew and Its Relation to Modern Antisemitism*. New Haven: Yale University Press, 1943.

Tuchman, Barbara. *A Distant Mirror: The Calamitous 14th Century*. New York: Knopf, 1978.

Ziegler, Philip. *The Black Death*. New York: John Day, 1969.